THE
FOOTSOLDIER

Martin Windrow & Richard Hook

Nothing except a battle lost can be half so melancholy as a battle won

Duke of Wellington   Dispatch from the field of Waterloo   June 1815

Oxford University Press 1982

Oxford University Press, Walton Street, Oxford OX2 6DP

London   Glasgow   New York   Toronto
Delhi   Bombay   Calcutta   Madras   Karachi
Nairobi   Dar es Salaam   Salisbury   Cape Town
Kuala Lumpur   Singapore   Hong Kong   Tokyo
Melbourne   Auckland

and associates in
Beirut   Berlin   Ibadan   Mexico City   Nicosia

ISBN 0 19 273147 5
Printed in Hong Kong

Contents

Timocrates of Athens
418 BC

We may suppose that groups of Stone Age hunter-gatherers fought one another over hunting territory and camping places far back in prehistory, but we cannot date our knowledge of true 'warfare' much earlier than about 3000 BC. For the purposes of this book we define a 'footsoldier' as a man fighting other men on foot, in a group organized for that reason, using weapons specifically designed for fighting, rather than hunting weapons or all-purpose tools, and dressed usually in protective or identifying clothing.

According to this definition, the appearance in history of the footsoldier took place some hundreds of years before the beginning of the Bronze Age in about 3000 BC. Before that date the use of copper for making implements and weapons was known in Egypt and Mesopotamia. But copper is a soft metal, of little use against a shield or another weapon. It was not until the technique of mixing copper and tin, to make the hard alloy bronze, began to spread across the Middle East that we see the common use of practical weapon blades—at first spears and axes, and later daggers and swords. By about 2500 BC the Sumerian people of

Mesopotamia were certainly using bronze-headed spears and axes and bronze-bladed knives. They wore bronze helmets and clothing with protective bronze plates, and fought in organized armies, drawn up in ranks of similarly-equipped soldiers.

In about 1200 BC the mining and working of iron, a much harder and more durable metal, was perfected. The first people to equip themselves with iron weapons and armour were the Assyrians, and this great advantage allowed them to dominate their part of the world for five centuries. In the 8th century BC their great king, the splendidly-named Tiglath-Pileser III, led them in the establishment of a large empire. The Assyrians were the first truly military nation of which we have knowledge; they had a strong central government, and a well-organized, permanent, 'standing' army.

It would be fascinating to know what the life of a soldier was like in one of those first Middle Eastern armies but our sources are so few and fragmentary that we can only guess. The earliest society which has left us a clear written record of the place of the soldier in society, and his way of life and death, is that of Classical Greece. It is there that we meet the footsoldier for the first time: in a marshy valley near the Arcadian town of Mantinea, on a summer's day in 418 BC . . .

For a moment the Spartan soldier facing Timocrates shifted his great shield, and exposed his unprotected throat beneath the rim of his helmet. Timocrates grunted with effort as he thrust at the few square inches of sun-tanned flesh, hefting his heavy eight-foot spear overarm. At the last second the Spartan lifted his shield again, and the spearhead thudded into it with an impact which made Timocrates's arm tingle. The point sheared through the thin bronze skinning of the shield and pierced deep into the wood and bull-hide. There it jammed, as Timocrates jerked urgently on the long, unwieldy shaft. He twisted and pulled at it in vain, as the probing point of the Spartan's own spear jabbed at the eye-holes in his helmet forcing Timocrates to duck and shift behind the rim of his own shield. He was hemmed in tightly on every side by shoving, stumbling, struggling men, and the long shaft was tangling in something behind him as he fought to free it. Then, just when he felt it begin to come free, a sword, thrust out of the confusion of clashing shields and bobbing helmets in front of him, with two ringing blows hacked his spear-shaft in two.

Unbalanced, Timocrates took an uncertain step backwards—and as he floundered, the point of the Spartan's spear came licking towards his chest. Instinc-tively he grabbed at it with his empty spear-hand, and hung on to the shaft just below the sharp head. The Spartan lunged on it again, almost tearing it free from Timocrates's sweating fingers. Forcing it a few inches further from his body, Timocrates looked around fran-tically for his right-hand comrade. If Hippias could occupy the Spartan, Timocrates could draw his own short-sword with his right hand, then push forward shield to shield, inside the enemy's guard, and stab round the shield-rim. But where *was* Hippias?

A moment ago he had been there, his familiar lion-painted shield a reassuring protection on Timo-crates's unguarded right side. Now he did not seem to be there any more, and—Zeus!—another Spartan was forcing his way forward into the gap in the front rank of the Athenian phalanx. Timocrates found it hard to make out clearly what was happening around him as he peered this way and that through the eye-holes of the deep helmet. It covered his ears, too, and the shouts, groans and clash of arms merged into a confused, echo-ing din. The Spartan heaved on the spear again, and the muscles of Timocrates's forearm jumped with the strain of holding it away. '*Hippias*! In the name of Athene!

On that summer's day, in the boggy valley east of Mount Maenalus, some 200 men of the thousand-

The heavy bronze body-armour used until the late 6th century BC was then replaced until c. 250 BC by a cuirass of layered and glued linen. Lightness and flexibility were its main advantages. A double split fringe across the hips and belly gave protection while allowing bending at the waist. It fastened on the left, where the join would be covered by the shield, and had a doubled shoulder-yoke. Although probably tougher than we might imagine, the 1/4-inch cloth was sometimes reinforced with metal scales at vulnerable points.

strong Athenian contingent fell under the Spartan spears. Whether or not one of them was Timocrates, son of Proteas of the district of Cholargus, all the dead men were examples of something quite new in the history of European warfare, something peculiar to Classical Greece. For the men fighting in the battle-line were not slaves or poor peasants. They were all to some degree wealthy and cultured gentlemen, fighting in the political interests of their city-state.

The Athenian gentleman

Timocrates, a man of thirty with a wife and two young sons, was a prosperous businessman as well as a trained soldier. He was one of about 40,000 citizens of Athens, out of a total population of perhaps 300,000 souls. His citizenship was hereditary. As a member of the upper class whose votes in elections decided the government and policy of the city, he accepted the obligation to defend the city with his own body when it was required. A gentleman of education and substance felt he owed an absolute duty to the city in which he lived such a rewarding life.

His family's wealth was largely founded by his grandfather. Branching out from the management of the family estates outside the city, he had acquired first one, and then a small flotilla of trading ships. His first merchant ventures had been limited to the produce of his own olive groves and fig orchards. By the time he died he had a prosperous business, exporting fine pottery, oil and manufactured items, and importing grain and linen from Egypt, and resin and pitch from the Black Sea ports. His son Proteas had proved a clever steward, and by the time Timocrates inherited the family fortune new ships, new estates, and an interest in the Laurium silver mines had been added. But it was not the Athenian way simply to devote one's life to commerce.

Since the age of seven, Timocrates had been given a broad education. He had been taught not only to read, write and calculate, but to appreciate the culture which made his city the envy of the civilized world. He knew by heart much of the writings of Homer, Hesiod, and Simonides. He could play the lyre, and had a fine ear for music. He had been taught the art of conversation and rhetoric, and was a sophisticated member of the city's social elite. He regularly gave dinner parties in his pleasant town house in the eastern suburbs of Athens, and around the couches one might hear the gossip of politics and commerce, the latest international news, and informed opinions of the currently fashionable artists and writers.

A fit and active body was as important to the Athenian as a witty and cultivated mind. As a boy Timocrates had spent as many hours in the gymnasium as at his books, and took pride in strengthening and exercising his body by competing in a number of sports.

Tactics for fighting in closely-ordered formation, and shield design, developed together. Unlike early types with a central hand-grip, hoplite shields of the 8th to 4th centuries BC had central loops for the forearm and hand-grips near the rim 1. The deep rim could be rested on the shoulder for most of the time 2. Both features allowed shields to be held in the same position for long periods, without tiring the soldier; the left half of each shield projected beyond the soldier's side, so his left-hand neighbour could 'pack in' tight behind it, allowing long ranks to form unbroken shield walls. Sometimes fabric or leather aprons were attached 3 to deflect or tangle arrows or spears aimed at the thigh. Swords were always worn, of simple form 4 or in the single-edged *kopis* shape 5, but the spear was the primary weapon.

With young manhood the gymnasium became as much a social club and debating society as a sports ground, but still Timocrates was careful to keep himself in good condition. In an age when men fought face to face with heavy weapons, an unfit soldier was dangerous to himself and his comrades.

The citizen militia

Like all the able-bodied young men of his age, Timocrates had been enrolled at seventeen as a cadet in one of the ten tribal regiments of Athenian heavy infantry. For two years he had learned the military skills. His father paid for his war-gear, and made sure he got the best. He was carefully fitted for the deep, skull-shaped helmet of bronze, made in the Corinthian style, which covered all but his eyes and mouth. His torso was protected by a cuirass made by gluing many layers of stiff cloth together, with a double fringe over hips and groin to allow easy movement. Thin bronze greaves, so well fitted that they clung exactly in place simply by the springiness of the metal, covered his shins. His main protection was a big round shield of bronze-covered wood and leather. One of his main tasks as a cadet was learning the proper handling of the shield with the left arm. In battle it covered him entirely from eyes to knees, and was far more important than the partial protection of the linen corselet.

Though every hoplite—heavy infantryman— carried an iron short-sword slung high under the left arm for close fighting and emergencies, Timocrates's main weapon was a heavy, eight-foot, iron-headed spear. During his cadet years he spent hours at a time practising with shield and spear—thrusting overarm and underarm; crouching with spear-butt braced on the ground, in static defence; running and leaping over obstacles in full gear, to strengthen the body and improve the agility. The close-order drill nearly drove him to tears of frustration before he mastered it. The hoplites fought in tightly-packed ranks—the phalanx—usually eight men deep from front to back, with companies of about 120 men drawn up side by side in a single long battle-line. Manoeuvring the long spear in such a formation without tripping over it, or jabbing the men behind with the sharp bronze-tipped butt, took a lot of practice.

During his two years' full-time military service Timocrates spent some time in the garrisons of outposts of the Athenian empire, both on the mainland and among the islands. Athens was a sea-going power, and her strength had been built on trade overseas. When he was nineteen he was released from the army and returned to civilian life, taking up the reins of his father's business, and in due course marrying, and fathering children. But he remained liable to be recalled

Most Greek battles were simple frontal clashes between long solid lines of hoplites, and won by the largest, freshest, most determined or luckiest. This simplified diagram shows an attacking phalanx **1** emerging from a defile and extending its front to match that of the waiting enemy phalanx **2**. A few cavalry **3** manoeuvre on or behind the wings, and lightly armed peasants skirmish in the hills **4**; neither has more than a limited supporting role. The hoplites' only 'tactic' was to avoid being outflanked by a longer enemy line. Each side tended to drift to the right in battle, as men unconsciously kept closing up behind the sheltering shield of their right-hand comrade. Thus there was a danger of having one's left wing outflanked, or of 'thin spots' appearing as the line stretched.

to the ranks in time of war until his sixtieth birthday; and in his lifetime, war was constantly breaking out. He served in three campaigns during his twenties, leaving Athens for a matter of weeks on each occasion—most fighting was limited to the summer months between seed-time and harvest.

In an emergency Athens could field some 30,000 hoplites, but to do so would have brought the life and business of the city to a standstill. Usually only those troops considered necessary for the task in hand were called to serve. They were organized into ten tribal 'regiments', but these were not actual battlefield units. Each contained a number of companies of about 120 men, the companies being of different age groups. Individual age groups of each regiment would be summoned as needed by the elected leaders of the city and army; the men in their prime formed the field army while the companies of young cadets and old veterans manned the fixed defensive garrisons.

At the time of Timocrates's life, Greece was troubled by a long-running series of campaigns between two of the most important of the hundred or so communities which inhabited the mainland and islands. Athens was a rich, sophisticated, cultured, outward-looking commercial state. Sparta was a brutal, deeply conservative military society, based on ruthless slavery

of the farm labour force, a society in which every citizen spent his adult life practising for and waging war. For years the two city-states fought and plotted against one another. Around them alliances of smaller city-states formed and broke and re-formed. In 418 BC Athens and Sparta were officially at peace, but both sent troops to the aid of their allies when trouble broke out in the area called the Peloponnese. Thus it was that 1,000 Athenian hoplites, including Timocrates son of Proteas, found themselves drawn up in the 4,000-man battle-line of the Argive League, outside Mantinea, facing a similar army of Spartans and Spartan allies. The spark for the campaign had been an age-old feud between the country townships of Mantinea and Tegea, but Timocrates knew he was really fighting another round in the struggle against the growth of Spartan power.

Into battle

The two armies spent some hours weighing each other up before the fighting started. Each was drawn up in a long line about eight ranks deep. Each commander wanted the other to attack first, since the defenders always enjoyed a slight advantage. Timocrates's company was near the left-hand end of the Argive line. Facing the Athenian contingent were the Spartans themselves, recognizable by the scarlet military cloaks

By eighty years after Mantinea the Macedonian kings, Philip and Alexander, had developed a much more sophisticated army. They created a balance between infantry and trained cavalry and made use of the strengths of each. The phalanx was now made up of —ideally—sixty-four units of some 250 men. They were drilled to adopt, and manoeuvre in, quite complex formations: arrowheads, curved and slanted lines, etc., depending on terrain and enemy battle-order. The Greek spear was replaced by a huge two-handed pike sixteen to twenty feet long; the shield hung from arm and neck straps. The pikes of the front five ranks thus protruded, making an impenetrable 'hedge' well in front of the soldiers; those of the other ranks stood up so thickly that they gave reasonable protection against arrows.

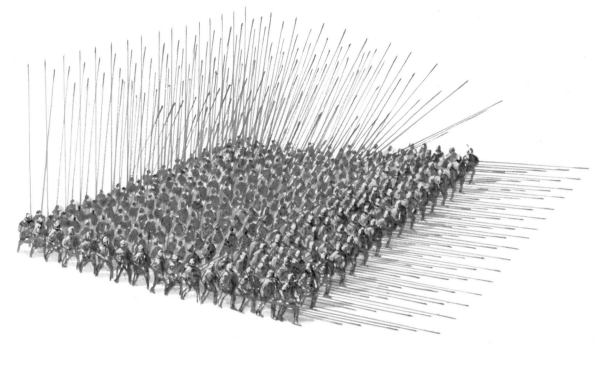

they threw off before forming up. Timocrates had no illusions about the Spartans. Their grim courage and endurance were legendary, and he had fought them before. At least, if the allies were defeated today, they would have a chance to run. Mantinea town was close by, and Greek armies seldom pursued a beaten enemy to destruction—the clear victory in battle was enough. In these continual campaigns there was a limit to what the city expected of its soldiers. Each man would fight bravely in the phalanx for as long as there was a chance of success, but if he was still alive when the day seemed lost and the line wavered, there was no shame in falling back and yielding the field.

While the two armies eyed one another across a few score yards of marshy ground, the generals made speeches to try and whip up the determination of their men. Timocrates had heard plenty of speeches, and did not need telling why he was there. The Spartans were singing their fierce war-songs, an uncomfortably impressive sound. Timocrates tried to think back to his leave-taking from his family. He had been up early on the appointed day, and had made the proper sacrifices to the gods for victory and protection. The beautifully clear early morning light had been streaming into the courtyard of his pleasant town house as his wife and eldest son helped him arm for the march. Cyneia had

been outwardly calm as she helped him lace his cuirass, and held ready the great polished shield with its dolphin blazon, traditional in his family since his grandfather had enjoyed such favour from the sea-god Poseidon. His little son Apollodorus had been glowing with pride as he held up the heavy helmet with its sweeping horse-hair plume. There had been no tears when he left the house with his body servants, and made his way to the assembly point in the great open square of the Agora. Gods grant he would see their beloved faces again soon . . .

There was a great shout, and along the front rank to his right he saw his officer, shining in a bronze cuirass modelled like a human torso, raise his spear in command. Timocrates took a quick look behind him, checking that the seven men of his file were properly in order. Then, to the shrilling of flutes, the battle-line of the Argive League began to tramp forward. As soon as they moved they saw the Spartans shimmer into motion as well, advancing in step to the measured music. The sun flashed on the long line of overlapping shields, and on the five hundred faceless bronze heads above them. Four thousand glittering spearheads came down into position, and eight of them were pointing directly at Timocrates as he walked steadily forward into the disastrous defeat of Mantinea.

Sextus Duratius of Legio II Augusta, 44 AD

After fighting one another to final exhaustion, the Greek city-states were absorbed in the 4th century BC by a great, if short-lived empire founded by the kings of Macedon, Philip and his legendary son Alexander. The Macedonian empire in its turn broke up and in 168 BC was decisively defeated by a vigorous new power—Rome.

Rome went on to build the greatest empire in world history. At first her armies were made up of citizen-volunteers serving in times of emergency, not unlike those of ancient Greece. But such armies are no use for long campaigns far from home, let alone for garrisoning the borders of a far-flung empire. By the 1st century AD a new sort of footsoldier dominated the Western world—a paid, trained, professional fighting man, serving in permanent regiments, and posted abroad at the order of a national government. Such a soldier might have been Sextus Duratius.

Panting from his scramble up the steep grassy slope, and from the short sharp fight with the tribesmen who had tried to hold it, Sextus Duratius paused to draw breath. The last of the Britons on this bank was down. For the moment the fighting had passed on ahead of Fronto's Century of the 2nd Cohort, Legio II Augusta.

Everything was going according to plan. Below and ahead of him Sextus saw the armoured backs and big red shields of Fatalis's Century pressing on through the sunken lane towards the gateway into the big Celtic hill-fort. Part of the century was in 'tortoise' formation, shields forming a box to protect the soldiers from the stones and javelins hurled by the howling tribesmen up on the ramparts. One or two legionaries were down. Probably the stones, thought Sextus: they were really more dangerous than soft native iron blades at this range. But the attack did not waver. Above the noise and the shouting Sextus thought he could hear the bull-bellow of Centurion Fatalis himself. Then the shield-box broke up, and the silver and red figures ran up the bank at their tormentors. To a soldier like Fatalis, twenty years with the legions, covered in scars and

decorations and wise to every trick of the frontier, it was just one more barbarian hill-village.

At a sudden whirring overhead Sextus ducked for a second, then straightened with a shame-faced grin. No catapults in *that* cattle-pen! It was the Augusta's own artillery changing targets. The Legate Vespasian was keeping his usual tight grip on the battle; as soon as these outer banks were signalled secure he would have ordered forward some of the legion's light mule-drawn catapults, to give close supporting fire for the final push through the gate. Vespasian was as much of a soldier as Centurion Fatalis, which made a change from the perfumed politicians who usually got commands.

Sextus looked around, as a hoarse grunting and mumbling behind him reassured him that old Cocles was safe. 'Getting a bit long in the tooth for foot-races?', he jeered affectionately, as the grizzled veteran panted up beside him. He was carrying his helmet, and blood

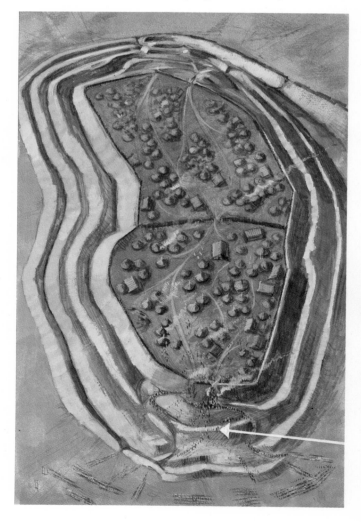

Mai-Dun, the huge neolithic hill-village near Dorchester, Dorset, now known as Maiden Castle. Man lived on this 1,000-yard long hill since at least 2000 BC. By 44 AD it enclosed the main village of the Durotrigian tribe and some 45 acres of ground. Huge earth ramparts, some 90 feet high, protected it in successive rings, and were strengthened at some points by dry-stone walls and timber pallisades. The west gate had seven different ramparts; even the east gate, chosen for attack by the Legio II Augusta, had four. Archaeologists have found dramatic evidence of the Roman storming of Mai-Dun.

from a grazed forehead trickled down his battered face. 'Look at that—best helmet I ever had, and not issued six months—now look at it!' The brow of the bright iron helmet was deeply gouged, and the decorative bronze piping curled out from its sprung rivets. 'Painted ape didn't know any better than to try a head-cut with his stupid great sword—no hope at all—and goes to his gods leaving me this mess for a legacy!' He muttered on, peering at the helmet with his one good eye and fiddling with the twisted bronze strip. Sextus turned back to the battle.

Through smoke from the burning huts he could see Fatalis and his lads almost inside the enclosure. Soon be over, he thought; once the legionaries were able to deploy into their proper ranks again inside the ramparts the Britons hadn't a hope. Discipline and training always beat individual courage. The Britons had no proper tactics, no professional officers, no armour, and pathetically old-fashioned weapons. They charged and slashed and hacked, but made little impression on that moving wall of Roman shields, Roman armour and helmets. Fatalis would put his lads in wedge formation, splitting up the enemy rush and crushing them into tight little groups where they couldn't swing their big soft swords. Then a bang in the face with the shield, and the long point of the wicked Roman short-sword stabbing up into their unarmoured bodies. A quick kick for luck, and on to the next, keeping alignment, keeping shields up, keeping comrades close each side, listening for the familiar signals from officers who were doing this job when you were a baby . . .

This must be the tenth—or eleventh?—of these forts that the Augusta and their attached auxiliary cohorts had taken since they first splashed ashore on this foggy island at the edge of the world. This was a good big one, all right—must be a mile long, and some of those ramparts were ninety feet high if he was any judge. Mai-Dun, it was called, but soon it would fall like the others, whose tongue-twisting names Sextus couldn't remember. What chance did these Britons have against the Augusta, which fought like a single great armoured animal, with 5,000 limbs; an animal directed by the cool professional Legate Vespasian, astride his horse with his staff officers and his messengers and trumpeters ready to relay his commands at every turn of the battle.

Things *could* go wrong. A Roman could slip on wet grass, just like anybody; he could misjudge his stroke, or get cut off and surrounded, and find himself answering roll-call among the Shades before he knew it. But

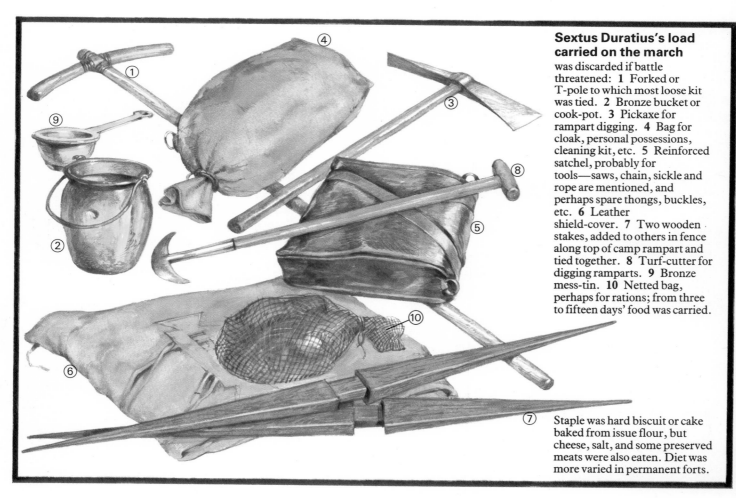

Sextus Duratius's load carried on the march was discarded if battle threatened: **1** Forked or T-pole to which most loose kit was tied. **2** Bronze bucket or cook-pot. **3** Pickaxe for rampart digging. **4** Bag for cloak, personal possessions, cleaning kit, etc. **5** Reinforced satchel, probably for tools—saws, chain, sickle and rope are mentioned, and perhaps spare thongs, buckles, etc. **6** Leather shield-cover. **7** Two wooden stakes, added to others in fence along top of camp rampart and tied together. **8** Turf-cutter for digging ramparts. **9** Bronze mess-tin. **10** Netted bag, perhaps for rations; from three to fifteen days' food was carried.

Staple was hard biscuit or cake baked from issue flour, but cheese, salt, and some preserved meats were also eaten. Diet was more varied in permanent forts.

Sextus Duratius's armour and weapons

were worn over a wool tunic and neck-scarf and perhaps, in winter, half-length trousers: **1** Curved rectangular shield made of three-ply wood covered with leather and linen, edged with bronze; the metal boss covered a countersunk hand-grip. On the march it was slung on a strap, and often protected with a leather cover. **2** Sextus probably carried two javelins. Roman attacks began with volleys of them; both light and weighted examples are known, perhaps for different ranges. The iron shank bent easily, preventing enemies pulling them out of their shields and throwing them back. Their shields were thus weighed down and unusable, leaving them unprotected when the legionaries closed to hand-to-hand range to fight with their swords. **3** Short stabbing sword, the shape copied from Spanish designs. Slung high on the right, it may have been drawn by pulling the hilt down and forward, so that the scabbard swung up under the armpit. **4** Legionary helmet of Imperial Gallic type: this iron pattern, shaped to protect skull, face and neck, replaced simpler bronze types shortly before Sextus sailed for Britain. The Roman army was very 'modern' in that equipment was mass-produced in factories all over the Empire according to approved patterns. Armour made in Gallic factories—modern France and the Rhineland west of the river—had a reputation for much higher quality than the products of Italian workshops, and archaeological finds bear this out. **5** Breast-and-back armour, of iron half-hoops mounted on internal straps and overlapping. This combined good protection and ease of movement. It was surprisingly light, and could be folded small enough to carry in a kit-bag. This armour replaced mail shirts in the legions early in the 1st century AD. **6** Belt reinforced with metal plates, carrying a dagger and a leather and metal groin-protector held in place by weights at the end of each strap. **7** The Roman legionary marched all over the known world in these famous 'boots'—heavy leather sandals with hob-nailed soles.

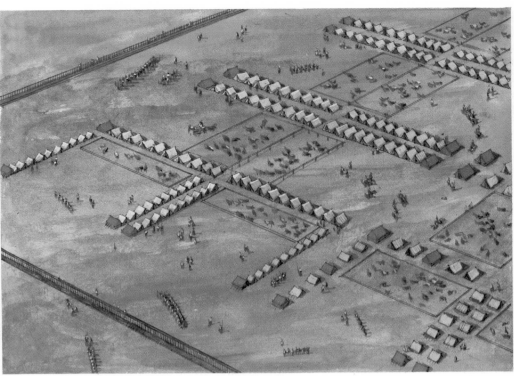

In war zones, all Roman units made a defended camp every night, with a ditch, a rampart and a fence. Camps were laid out identically according to official patterns and measurements. The relative positions of each unit's tents, the headquarters, the baggage areas, the four gates and the various roadways never changed. In theory, a soldier could find his way blind-fold around any camp, from Syria to Hadrian's Wall. Camping was thus a quick, efficient routine, and there was less chance of confusion if attacked at night.

with officers who knew their business, and comrades who kept an eye on your back, the odds were quite good enough for Sextus, who was a gambler by nature.

His father was a time-expired legionary of the Augusta who ran a wine-shop outside its great stone fortress at Strasbourg. When Sextus was seventeen the old man got fed up with him loafing around the tavern with the drinkers, dicing away hard-earned money, and sent him up to the headquarters with a note for his old comrade Fronto, now senior centurion of the 2nd Cohort. Being strong, fit, a Roman citizen, and the son of a respected ex-soldier and local businessman, Sextus soon found himself taking the oath to the Emperor before the awe-inspiring eagle standard of the 2nd Augusta. For the next twenty-five years, sickness, luck, and barbarian spears permitting, he would be a soldier of the legion.

As a soldier, in what he considered the finest legion in the Empire, Sextus could hope for travel, adventure, and promotion: promotion, perhaps, to the unapproachable godlike status of a senior centurion, commanding a cohort of 500 men. In return for hard knocks and unquestioning obedience he would receive 337½ silver pennies a year, in three instalments—less compulsory deductions for rations, boots, replacement of lost kit, burial insurance, and anything else the penny-pinching clerks could think up. He might get handsome bonuses from time to time—if he was in an important victory, or if a new Emperor came to power. Part of his pay would be safely banked for him, and if he survived his term of enlistment he would get a generous lump-sum pension, or a grant of land instead. It was not at all a bad deal—provided you lived to collect on it.

During the first months Sextus often doubted that he would survive his first year. He learned the soldier's trade the hard way, harried about the parade ground and practice field by the brazen tongues and vine-wood cudgels of the instructing centurions. He learned how to keep his armour clean and bright, even if it meant sitting up half the night. He learned how to march twenty-five miles a day in full kit, rain or shine, with hob-nailed sandals raising blisters on his blisters. As often as not he reeled back to barracks only to be herded straight off to the practice ground to dig ditches and build ramparts—and to see them filled in again, ready for tomorrow's session. He learned to handle javelin, sword and shield. He suffered more bruises and grazes than he could count from the double-weight wooden swords they practised with before being trusted with Roman steel in their shaky hands. He learned to recognise the signals for the different battle formations—the 'wedge', the 'saw', and all the other tricks of combat. And he learned just who, when, and how much to bribe, in order to avoid the frequent appearance of his name on the centurion's little lists for latrine-cleaning, cookhouse-cleaning, camp-cleaning, and a dozen other traps for the unwary recruit. Before two years had passed he was a thoroughly trained, disciplined, and dangerous professional soldier.

It had been eight years before Sextus and his comrades started their long journey by foot and barge and ship from the familiar surroundings of Strasbourg, with its stone barracks and lively civilian town, to the empty beaches and rolling, forested hills of Britain. In that time he had served on two or three short local expeditions on the German frontier—nothing serious, not much more than tax-gathering trips enlivened by the occasional brisk skirmish. He discovered that his training really worked, and that gave him confidence.

He had needed it, on this rather frightening expedition into the far northern mists. Only the gods knew what horrors awaited a man in these black woods and wind-haunted uplands, to say nothing of the dangers of drowning in the choppy grey seas or dying under the spears of the Britons. They were only savages, of course, but there had been a lot of them, in some of the early battles of the invasion. But the magic of Roman arms and discipline worked again, and Sextus soon forgot his doubts and fears.

When the Augusta was detached from the other legions and marched westwards things improved even more. Away from the eyes of the generals and staff officers, the Legate Vespasian proved a fair and decent commander. He expected his legionaries to do their duty, and do it quickly and thoroughly; but he didn't nag at men who were fighting almost every day.

Tonight, for instance, when the battle was over— and to judge from the thickening smoke and the noise from beyond the gateway it wouldn't be long now— Sextus could hope for a good night's rest. Perhaps the auxiliary cohorts which hadn't been in action would be ordered to dig the ramparts and pitch the tents for the men who had fought today? At any rate, Sextus probably wouldn't have to stand guard.

He looked forward to the familiar routine of evening in camp, sweetened by the excitement of victory, and a generous wine-ration for the victors. He could sit under the summer stars in front of the squad tent, warming his feet by the cooking fire and eating griddle-cakes—not to mention the pigeons old Cocles had bought from one of the 'tame' native scouts who accompanied them. The eight legionaries of his mess hadn't suffered any casualties today—you couldn't count old Cocles's scratched head, or Rufus's sliced arm—so there would be nothing to damp down the mood. Comradeship, a full belly, the tiredness of a job well done, and the familiar routine of soldiering—a good sleeping-draught for a strong man.

Gilderic the Frank, 620 AD

By the time the Roman Empire in the West collapsed in 406 AD, swamped by a migrating horde of barbarians who poured across the frozen Rhine, the superb army in which Sextus Duratius had served was already a distant memory. Continual civil wars, corruption, treachery, lack of money, and the widespread use of barbarian mercenaries had buried the old legionary spirit. The rag-tag armies scraped together by the last Emperors of the West did not differ greatly from the armies which defeated them.

Many of the barbarian invaders now fought from horseback. These cavalry armies lacked organization and discipline, but they moved forward with the grim determination of migrating peoples, and the infantry of Rome could not stand against them.

Centuries of turmoil followed, as barbarian kingdoms were carved out of the remains of the Empire. These kingdoms fought among themselves, disappeared in their turn, and were replaced by new waves of tribesmen. By about the 7th century a pattern of permanent settlement began to emerge. Professional armies were gone beyond memory. Men now fought in war-bands gathered around local leaders, for loot and for their chieftain's gifts. We may imagine one of these war-parties in action somewhere in northern France, on a winter's morning early in the 7th century, and among them, one named Gilderic . . .

The blazing thatch of the little wattle-and-daub house crackled fiercely, fanned by the cold dawn wind. Gilderic and his comrades howled in triumph, and beat their weapons against their shields. Around them in the trampled, blood-stained snow lay about a score of their enemies. The village headman and his last few fighting men had retreated into this house as Count Dagobert's warriors closed in on them. Dagobert had ordered the roof fired, and soon they would be forced out into the open to face the spears.

Gilderic jostled forward, shoving comrades out of his way in his eagerness to reach the front of the crowd facing the door. He had killed several defenders already, his blood was up, and he was determined to show his loyalty and courage in the only way which mattered—by standing shoulder-to-shoulder with his leader in the battlefront. This raid was long-planned, a calculated attack to wipe out an insult to Dagobert's authority, and he would be generous in victory. The captured war-gear would be distributed among his warriors, and the headman had been wielding a fine Elbe sword, its hilt decorated with gold, and crimson garnets. It would belong to the man who killed him. Gilderic badly wanted that sword.

Dagobert was the count of a wide area of Eastern Frankland. He had been appointed by a weak and far-off king, and had made himself virtually an independent monarch in his own lands. He was war-leader, law-giver, and tax-collector. He had given Gilderic a little farm, and authority over a family of peasants who worked it. Its produce fed Gilderic's family and the peasants, and left a small surplus which provided Gilderic's arms, and allowed him the freedom to serve Dagobert as a soldier when summoned. He had fought in several summer campaigns already, winning renown in the war-band by his courage and energy. This was the first time he had ever been summoned in winter—to fight in winter was a thing almost unknown. Travel was difficult, food was short, and all sensible men spent the cold months at home, tending their farms and mending their gear beside warm fires.

Dagobert had been feuding with a neighbouring count for some time over a strip of territory which divided their counties. The wording of the king's land grant was not clear and while Latin-speaking secretaries argued at the far-off court, Dagobert and Count Theodast pursued their quarrel in more direct ways. Dagobert's patience had finally snapped last harvest-

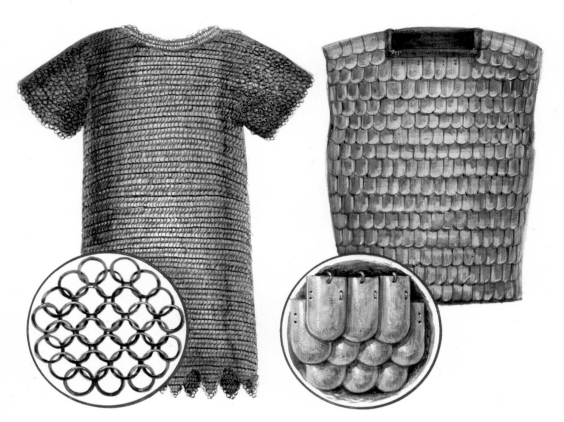

time, when some of Theodast's men killed one of his tax-gatherers in the main village of the disputed territory. Cunningly biding his time until winter isolated every little community in its forest clearing, Dagobert now hit back without mercy. To tolerate the death of his servant without revenge was unthinkable; it struck at the very basis of his power.

The Count had summoned nearly a hundred of his most reliable freemen, Gilderic among them. Marching as fast as the snow allowed, they had crossed the border of Dagobert's land. One night was spent huddled miserably around little fires in some old Roman ruins, with only cold barley-cakes and dried stock-fish to eat. The second night was worse. They were too close to their prey to light fires, and few of the warriors got any sleep as they crouched among the treetrunks bundled in their cloaks and furs. Dawn found them hidden along the edge of the trees, looking down at the sleeping village.

It was quite large—bigger than Gilderic's little hamlet of half-a-dozen cottages. He could see a score of thatched houses and sheds grouped around a timber-framed hall which must belong to the headman. There was even a tiny stone and timber church. Gilderic muttered a prayer for victory under his breath. Then, for good measure, another to Thor and Woden.

It was Gilderic who noticed a stretch of the stockade where the villagers had carelessly allowed the wind to pile up a deep snowdrift. Frozen hard, it made a natural ramp almost to the top of the pallisade. He pointed it out to Dagobert, and was rewarded with a grin and a slap on the shoulder. It was Gilderic, too,

who dropped over the stockade first, and who clubbed the snarling guard-dog silent. At Dagobert's shoulder he ran across the open ground towards the first houses.

It was a short, murderous little battle. The villagers tumbled out of doors, gummy-eyed with sleep and only half armed, to meet the stabbing javelins and thrown axes of Dagobert's followers. There was no formal order, and no tactics beyond a rough and ready attempt to fight in some kind of a line, to avoid being outflanked in the lanes between the cottages. Each man simply rushed at the enemy facing him, and a dozen hand-to-hand duels with spear, sword and axe broke out at once.

No quarter was asked nor given. Every grown male in the village was marked for death. It was not surprising that some of the village slaves chose to fight beside their masters, picking up discarded weapons or clubbing wildly with farm tools. One red-haired giant, stark naked except for the iron slave-ring round his neck, nearly brained Gilderic with a spade as he was trying to free the barbs of his javelin from the ribs of a fallen enemy. He was warned by the slave's outlandish northern war-cry, and managed to take the force of the blow on his wooden shield and iron cap; his head rang with it for some time after. He ham-strung the slave with his belt-axe, and finished him off with the javelin.

Winners and losers

With a crash and a shower of sparks and blackened thatch the roof of the cottage collapsed. There was a shout of pain from inside. Then the door was unbarred

Warriors of the Dark Ages

From the 4th to 11th centuries Europe was a melting-pot of peoples, and thus of war-gear designs. No hard divisions can be drawn between races; nor did styles develop in any rigid series of steps. What evidence we have shows both differences and similarities between warriors widely distant in time and place:

1 4th century Roman soldier His appearance owes more to the Central European tribes he fought, and among whom he was increasingly recruited, than to the 1st century legionary.

2 6th century 'Vendel' warrior From grave finds in Sweden we can reconstruct this striking helmet—not totally unlike the late Roman type—and this interesting splinted limb armour. **3 9th century Viking warrior** Helmets with iron 'spectacle' eye-guards recall Vendel type. The horned or winged helmet beloved of Victorian romantic artists was pure fiction. Quality of clothing was far higher than once believed—Vikings were sophisticated world travellers and traders, not merely barbarian pirates. **4 9th century Saxon warrior** Plain iron caps, ring-mail, round shields, spears and broadswords were probably the most common war-gear throughout the West for many centuries. 'Saxons' and 'Vikings' were simply earlier and later waves of immigrants from neighbouring and similar cultures. **5 9th century Frankish soldier** Evidence is patchy, but we may guess at some kind of crested helmet; scale armour was certainly worn. **6 11th century Norman** This third-generation Viking settler shows Norse origins in his 'spangenhelm', and perhaps Byzantine influence in the kite-shaped shield. Long mail coats and leggings became the norm in Europe. After settling among the Franks the Norseman copied them in taking to the horse; this warrior is the direct ancestor of the medieval knight.

Surviving remains of many helmets show that the skills of plate-metal smiths were not lost although plate body armour was abandoned.

and thrown open, and the headman and three other warriors charged out, to make an end of it in the open.

The headman was obviously quite wealthy. He wore a shirt of ring-mail, and that sword must be worth the price of a horse. He came straight for Gilderic, red-eyed and scorched but still full of fight. The mail shirt was going to be a problem . . . But even as Gilderic was parrying sword-blows with the iron shaft of his javelin, a struggling knot of fighters stumbled into them and swept them apart. Gilderic tried to reach him again, but was too late—Count Dagobert himself cut down the headman with an axe-stroke which sheared right through shield-rim and neck. The last of the defenders went down under half-a-dozen spear-thrusts, and it was all over.

Two hours later Dagobert's war-band assembled for the journey home. They had lost five dead and two others too badly wounded to be carried. Dead and wounded alike had been left in the care of the terrified little priest, who had watched the raid from the windows of the tiny church. A gold piece had secured the promise of decent burial and the right words spoken over their dead; but whether the quaking cleric would be able to protect the wounded from Count Theodast's furious horsemen when they arrived at the scene of the massacre was less certain. That was a risk a warrior took, and Gilderic did not dwell on it.

Smoke was still rising from the burnt-out cottage as the little army trudged out of the village towards the concealing forest. Dagobert had not burned the rest of the houses—after all, he intended to add this place to his own lands. As he rode at the head of his warriors he was already planning a summer campaign on a larger scale. This raid would bring him prestige. The cattle, chests of seed-corn, and captured weapons would encourage his followers. It was always hard to keep a sizeable force in the field for any length of time, even in summer—his authority depended upon a blend of fear, admiration and popularity, and hot-headed fighting men tended to have short memories. Still, they were happy enough to follow him now.

Gilderic was certainly happy as he stalked proudly at his Count's stirrup. His few trifling cuts had been staunched with rags soaked in snow-water. His wallet was heavy with silver coins, dug from the usual hiding place under the hearth of the village headman's hall. He was already looking forward to the pleasure of boasting of his exploits to his wife, his peasants, and his young son. His share of the common booty ought to amount to a goat or two and some grain—not to be despised in these hungry months. And best of all, Dagobert had presented him with the fine Elbe sword, decorated with gold and garnets, as reward for leading the way over the stockade. He strode towards the trees among his singing companions—watched by the widows and orphans huddled in the blood-stained snow.

These reconstructions show:
1 Decorative helmet of 7th century Saxon king from Sutton Hoo, Suffolk. **2** Saxon helmet with iron frame and horn plates, bearing both pagan boar symbol and Christian cross, from Benty Grange, Derbyshire. **3** Gilded bronze 7th century helmet from Morken, near Cologne. **4** Iron and bronze 6th century helmet of 'Vendel culture' from Uppland, Sweden. **5** Traditionally, 'St. Wenceslas's helmet', preserved in Prague: 10th century. This 'spangenhelm' shape was seen all over Europe.

Soldiers of Byzantium

After Rome's collapse in the West, the Eastern Empire lived on as an independent, isolated power based on Byzantium (Constantinople). Only here did the sophisticated organization of the old Roman standing army survive. **1** The 11th century Byzantine spearman served in a permanent regiment, identified by plume and shield design. Note mixture of scale, ring, and splinted armour. Byzantium, learning from contact with other peoples, developed in its own way. Among its many mercenary soldiers were the Vikings of the famous 'Varangian Guard' **2**. This guardsman wears ornate silk parade dress of Byzantine style but retains the great battle-axe which became the 'trademark' of the Norseman.

Ottocar of Lubeck, 1191

The importance of the horse-soldier increased steadily from the 8th to the 11th century. At first it was his mobility which made him valuable: cavalry could sometimes catch and beat the hit-and-run raiders from the fringes of Western Europe who harrassed the settled kingdoms during this period. As time passed, and new armour and tactics were developed, the mounted man became the lord of the battlefield. The introduction of stirrups gave him a firm seat on his horse. Now he could brace a spear under his arm and charge full-tilt at his enemy, using the shock and weight of impact. Protected by a long coat of mail and a kite–shaped shield, the rider became almost invulnerable to infantry. The footsoldier's position declined until he was almost disregarded in a pitched battle.

Only a wealthy landowner could afford to equip himself for battle. In order to build up their cavalry, kings gave their nobles large estates in return for military service. The common people became serfs—little more than slaves, bound to work their lord's land for life. Despised, ill-equipped and untrained, the footsoldier played little part in warfare except for manning castle garrisons.

In the 12th century, however, there were occasional campaigns which showed that if used properly by an imaginative commander, infantry could at least give the all-important mounted knights useful support. This was true of the Crusades, the series of long wars in which European armies tried to drive the Muslims from the Holy Land of Palestine.

Ottocar and a few others broke ranks and stumbled out of the dust of the marching column towards the well they had spied amidst the village ruins. Behind them they heard hoof-beats and hoarse shouts of protest. The Norman sergeant reined up by the knot of grimy footsoldiers clustered round the well, shouting orders in his foreign tongue, and pointing back to their company as it straggled past. His meaning was clear enough, whatever the language. The English king commanding this great allied army on its march down from Acre towards the Holy City had enforced a discipline even Ottocar's old Emperor would have approved. No straggling, no foraging, and above all, no breaking ranks.

The infantry were to form a screen of spearmen and crossbowmen all along the flanks and rear, shielding the precious knights and their horses in the centre from the swirling attacks of the enemy horse-archers. The Muslims were terrible foes, but they respected the crossbowmen from Italy and Germany. They had learned the hard way that the short, smashing bolts from the mechanical bows could knock a horse over at a hundred yards, a range at which most of the light arrows from the Muslims' hand-bows plucked uselessly at the shields and quilted jerkins of the Christian soldiers.

The Norman sergeant was evidently no stranger to the crossbow, either. When a group of Genoese foot-soldiers turned from the well and raised their weapons with a mutinous growl, he gave up and rode back towards the column, cursing and shaking his fist. Ottocar grunted with satisfaction, and went on sluicing the brackish water over his burning face and neck, using his iron 'kettle-helmet' as a bowl. After two and a half years of marching and fighting, he was within days of the Holy Sepulchre itself. One more battle, and he would be treading Christ's steps in the streets of Jerusalem.

A breeze sprang up from the west, the direction of the coast, where the Crusaders' fleet was following their line of march. Ottocar rested for a few moments, easing his cramped and sweating shoulders under the heavy mailshirt and quilted jerkin. The great army was struggling on past him in an endless column, raising choking clouds of brown dust. In the centre rode massed squadrons of mail-clad knights on strong warhorses, their lances gay with coloured pennons. If the

Crusader crossbowmen and spearmen fought in pairs, the bowman shooting from the shelter of the spearman's braced shield and levelled spear. Horses would not 'charge home' against spears. By 1250 the tactic was common in Europe. Padded buckram jerkins gave good protection even without mail: witnesses recalled men marching on, unconcerned, with up to ten arrows stuck in the thick quilting.

nimble, lightly-armed Muslim cavalry could be brought to battle in a place where they had to stand and fight, instead of stinging and then whirling away like flies, the weight of the knights' charge would crush them utterly. But the worshippers of Mohammed would seldom stand and fight. They used their mobility and speed to ambush, to surround, to harrass, to drive or lure the Christians into treacherous country far from water, where they could be separated and picked off.

It was to avoid this fate, which had befallen so many Crusader armies, that King Richard of England was so insistent on march-discipline. Companies of spearmen and crossbowmen trudged along together on both sides of the mounted squadrons. The horsemen were forbidden to react to Muslim harrassment by charging out of the column. When the brightly-robed heathen came swirling out of the dust, firing arrows in an attempt to unhorse the knights and leave them helpless on foot, Ottocar and his comrades moved outwards from the column and made a human wall to protect the horses. Each crossbowman crouched under the protection of the braced shield and shaft of a spearman, and the buzzing crossbow-bolts soon deterred the lightly armoured enemy. Ottocar could quite see the sense in this method. Without the mounted knights to win pitched battles, footsoldiers were doomed. But it was a weary way of fighting across this parched land, and a dangerous one. There had been days when he plucked half-a-dozen slim arrows out of his thick buckram jerkin after an enemy raid; it would only take bad luck for one to pierce his face or an unprotected limb, and in this heat a wound turned bad within hours. He had come such a long, wretched way to see the Holy Sepulchre; he prayed he would not stop a Muslim arrow now, so close at last.

Of the 30,000 German Crusaders who had marched from Ratisbon in May 1189, Ottocar was one of scarcely 1,000 who still marched under the banner of Christ.

Led by their Emperor, Frederick Redbeard of the house of Hohenstaufen, the Crusaders had set out to march across country to the Holy Land. At first all had gone well. Their old Emperor was a great general and a stern disciplinarian, and he had kept the army together and in good order, but as they made their way through the mountains of Bulgaria and Serbia things began to go wrong. There were great storms, terrible roads, brigand ambushes, and treachery by the Greeks who were supposed to rule that wild land. Men and horses had started to perish by the roadside in ever-growing numbers. Somehow their old Emperor had kept them going, and had obtained safe passage from Greece into Asia. But then the Turks, too, broke their word, and for three months the dwindling army crept through desolate mountains—starving, parched by day, frozen by night, and reduced to cooking foundered war-horses over fires

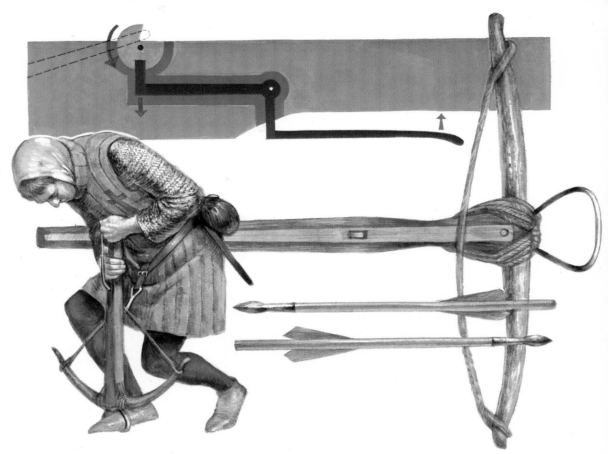

'An unchristian weapon'
Crossbows were short, thick bows mounted on a wooden butt. They shot short, heavy 'bolts' with enough force to pierce any armour at fifty yards. Stiffness made them hard to pull; by the late 12th century bowmen used a belt-hook and stirrup, forcing the string back by straightening their body. The string was hooked on a pivotting nut held in place by a pivotting trigger-bar. By pulling up the end of the bar the bowman freed the nut to rotate, releasing the string. Later iron crossbows, needing mechanical loading devices, became dangerously slow to use—their main disadvantage against the simple longbow. Nevertheless, their accuracy and penetrating power made them very useful weapons for troops such as castle garrisons, who were not in danger of being overrun while they reloaded.

made of tents and even spear-shafts. Then, within sight of rest and comfort in friendly Armenia, Frederick had died of a seizure. Without him the army began to dissolve. Some lords gave up and turned back; others led their surviving men off on expeditions of their own, forgetting their vow to capture the Holy City or die in the attempt. Ottocar's lord, Count Adolf of Holstein, had been one of those who pressed on, and finally joined the rest of the multi-national Crusader army in the disease-ridden siege-lines before Acre at the end of 1190. Ottocar had his own reasons for being glad of that.

He was quite an old man now, over 50 years old, and he had been a soldier all his life. Born on the lands of Count Adolf's father, near Lübeck on the Baltic coast of Germany, he was the son of a serf. In Germany, unlike most other European countries, there was a long tradition of serfs serving not merely as peasant farmers, bound for life to till their lords' fields, but as paid soldiers. Ottocar had gone wherever he was sent, fighting his lord's wars, and his Emperor's. He had served in the garrisons of castles on the wild eastern frontier, in cruel forest campaigns against the pagan Slavs. He had fought in civil wars against the dukes of Saxony. He had followed Frederick Redbeard on foreign campaigns, against Poles and Italians and Hungarians. More than once he had fought against the troops of the Pope himself. And that was the reason he was dreaming of Jerusalem.

Ottocar believed absolutely in Heaven and Hell. He knew he had committed many sins in his life; he had done cruel things and watched unmoved while others did worse. He was becoming very afraid, as his life passed through middle age, that his soul would burn in Hellfire forever. There was also the matter of the crossbow. Two successive Popes had declared it an evil and sinful weapon, not to be used against Christians; one German king had banned it from his armies. The knights and nobles hated it; in the hands of a common soldier it was deadly to a great lord, no matter how good his ring-mail. But it was so effective that they still allowed its use against their enemies; Ottocar—who had a steady hand and a straight eye—had killed dozens of men with the crossbow, and his soul lay in mortal danger because of it.

But the Pope had promised the Crusaders that by risking all in the service of Christ, to recapture the Holy Places of Our Lord's life and passion, they would gain absolution from all their sins. Ottocar believed that by killing unbelieving dogs of Muslims he was winning for himself eternal bliss in Heaven. And so he slouched on towards Jerusalem, braving danger and misery, happy in his simple faith that he could wade through blood to the throne of the gentle Christ. The knights would get there first, of course, but a priest had assured him that there would be a place in Paradise even for a sinful old crossbowman.

Seth of Tildesley
1415

At about the same time as the German and Italian crossbowmen were proving their worth on the Third Crusade, a Welsh churchman recorded that the Anglo-Norman lords who were fighting to tame the wild frontiersmen of his country were encountering skilled and dangerous archers armed with the simple, hand-held wooden bow. In the 13th century the prowess of Welsh archers became famous in England. Increasingly the Plantagenet warrior-kings recruited these useful soldiers for their own campaigns. In 1298 King Edward I won a decisive victory at Falkirk over the Scots by the use of massed longbowmen. Throughout the 14th century the importance of the bowman increased in England. The government encouraged English peasants to learn and practise the skills of archery, going so far as to ban any other sport on Sundays and feast-days. By recruiting archers in their thousands, and paying them good wages, King Edward III and his son the Black Prince, on their many expeditions to France, cancelled out the great advantage in numbers of armoured knights enjoyed by the enemy.

The French had few disciplined infantry, and considered battle to be the exclusive and honourable business of aristocratic armoured cavalry. They despised archers as their social inferiors, and for many years did not bother to develop tactics to defeat them. Again and again—notably at Crécy in 1346 and Poitiers in 1356—large French armies of knights and men-at-arms were slaughtered by smaller English armies in which bowmen outnumbered knights by three or four to one. Typically, the English picked a defensive position which would force the proud French chivalry to charge them on a narrow front. The English knights dismounted and formed a battle-line with masses of archers on the flanks and at various other points on their front. The French would charge, only to have their horses slaughtered by the English arrows, the riders thinned and weakened before they could come to sword's-length with the waiting English. When the French countered this by advancing dismounted, in full armour, to fight the English knights on equal terms, they found that at close range the great English warbow could send arrows even through plate steel. Despite the lessons of Crécy and Poitiers, which ruined French power for a generation, very much the same thing happened in 1415 when the young King Henry V of England led an army to France once more. The moment of truth came on the twenty-fifth of October, in a muddy field between the villages of Tramecourt and Agincourt, south of Calais.

Seth stood in position on the left of the pitifully small English battle-line. When he saw the great squadron of glittering French knights couch their lances, set spurs to their chargers, and begin to roll across the mud which separated the armies, he was almost glad. He was probably going to die—but at least the thing would be over, one way or another, and he was grimly determined to show those proud popinjays what a Lancaster archer could do, before he was cut down. It was better to die bow in hand, face to face with the enemy, than to perish of hunger and disease by some muddy trackside in the chill October drizzle.

The campaign had started with high hopes, but everything had gone wrong, almost from the start. The English army had landed on the French coast on the fourteenth of August, with the plan of capturing the port of Harfleur as a supply base, and then striking inland towards Paris. But the brave French garrison had held out behind their moat and strong walls for far longer than had been thought possible. For more than a month the siege had kept King Henry's army pinned down in the unhealthy marshland. More men were lost to the disease which soon swept through the camp than to French blades in the repeated assaults on the town walls. By the time Harfleur surrendered on the twenty-second of September over 2,000 of the English had died, from the great Earl of Suffolk down to humble archers. Some 5,000 others were so weak with dysentery that they were shipped home to England.

The campaigning season was far advanced, and it

The killing ground
English armies of the Hundred Years' War, usually outnumbered, picked defensive positions when possible. This illustrates an 'ideal' battle-line: **1,2** Woods and marshes guard flanks, and limit the enemy's frontage for attack. **3** If time allowed, holes were dug to break horses' legs and trip knights. **4** Armoured knights dismounted to fight with swords, axes, pole-arms or lances. **5** Wedges of archers, with stakes as protection against cavalry, were able to shoot forwards and inwards, channelling an enemy on to the narrow fronts of the divisions of dismounted knights. Few of the enemy could use their weapons at any one moment. **6** King or other commander placed with a clear view of the battle, with a small reserve of mounted knights for counter attack if necessary.

was rumoured in the camps that many of King Henry's council were advising him to abandon his plan for a march inland, and to be content with garrisoning Harfleur as a base for another expedition in the spring. But the king was determined to make some sort of demonstration that he could march at will through territory which he claimed as his own by right, and others among his lords supported him. It was decided that there was little risk in a quick march north-east to Calais, another English-held port, less than 200 miles away. So on the eighth of October about 1,000 knights and men-at-arms and some 5,000 archers set out from Harfleur. They took only the lightest baggage on their pack-horses, and rations for just eight days' march. Little did they know that the journey would take more than twice that time, for only forty miles south of their planned route a huge French army was gathering to cut them off.

The march had been a disaster. In constant rain the sickly little army trudged northwards and eastwards, their hopes fixed on Calais and safety rather than on battle. But the French scouting parties were everywhere. The English were forced to turn south along the river Somme, marching further and further from the coast and safety, in their search for a crossing. By the time they managed to ford the river a mighty French army had crossed their path and was somewhere ahead of them, barring their road to Calais. A wide track of ground torn up by the hooves of thousands of horses

betrayed the presence of the huge force on the move ahead of them. Chilled, exhausted, their rations gone, the little column struggled on into ever greater danger; there was nowhere else to go.

Seth had been tempted to lie down in the mud and go to sleep, many times during the seventeen cruel days of that march. He was weak with dysentery, and during the second half of the march his only food was a few vegetables grubbed up from fields and eaten raw. This was his first taste of war, and his bright dreams of glory and French gold were far away now. But he was kept on his feet by his comrade John, an experienced old archer from the same village who had served with the English garrison of Bordeaux. He was not a gentle nurse, but his kicks and curses and rough encouragement kept Seth moving. John had warned him, more than once, that the French had promised to hack off the right thumb and first two fingers of every English bowman they captured to prevent him ever drawing a bow again. The thought of capture and mutilation was worse than the prospect of shivering himself to death in a French cow-byre; so Seth had kept moving, somehow.

They had finally come up with the French last night—a great, sprawling host of knights, their armour gleaming dully in the overcast evening light like a shoal of fish, their banners and coat-armour gay with every colour and blazon of French heraldry. They were camped across the shallow valley in a silken city of tents and pavilions, bright with fires and torches and loud with song. There must have been 25,000 of them, all confident of victory, all promising a bloody revenge for past defeats.

In the orchards and copses around the hamlet of Maisoncelles the little band of tattered English had spent a chill and hungry night; many believed it would be their last, and Seth had not been the only one who passed the hours of darkness more in prayer than in rest.

In the cold light of a wet dawn they had taken up their positions in a muddy ploughed field, their thin line blocking the gentle slope between two belts of woodland. King Henry had ridden up and down, encouraging them to fight for England's honour and their own. Then, after a miserable wait in the drizzle, when it was obvious that the huge French army was in no hurry to attack, they had been ordered to walk forward until they were at extreme bow-shot from the enemy first line. There they had hammered into the ground the sharpened stakes which they had carried on the march as a defence against surprise attack. There they had pulled their bows in the first volleys of the battle, hoping to sting the French into charging. And it had worked. The enemy were drawn up in three great masses of dismounted knights, one behind the other. On their flanks were strong squadrons of cavalry. When the stinging arrows began to fall among them these proud horsemen urged their mounts forward, the right flank squadron riding straight at the wedge of English archers standing among their stakes on the edge of the woods of Agincourt.

Seth set his feet firmly in the heavy clay, drew a clothyard arrow from the sheaf of twenty-four stuck in the ground ready to his hand, and nocked and pulled in one practised motion. His six-foot bow of Spanish yew bent in a half-circle as his powerful shoulders and arms pulled a weight of more than a hundred pounds. Then he loosed, and the heavy ash shaft, tipped with a hardened steel 'bodkin' head, flew to meet the enemy— just one shaft among perhaps 2,000 which were crossing the shortening distance between the armies at that instant. Seth did not pause to watch its fall, but reached, nocked, and loosed again. He could fire ten arrows in a minute and so could every one of the 5,000 English archers on the field. In the minute-and-a-half it took the French mounted squadrons to reach the English line between 25,000 and 50,000 shafts were loosed at them—a hissing, clattering, steel-tipped hailstorm, which pincushioned horses and hurled their armoured riders to the ground. As the range closed even the sheet steel of the French armour could not protect its wearers. Here and there an arrow, striking true, punched straight through breastplate or visor. Where the long, tapered 'bodkins' struck the ring-mail covering armpit, throat or groin they pierced it as if it were

paper, goring deeply through leather and cloth and into the flesh beneath. The French horsemen withered, and dwindled, and turned back like a spent wave from a beach. The handful of riders who reached the hedgehog of pointed stakes were dragged from their screaming horses and butchered by archers who fell on them in mobs, stabbing through eye-slits or mailed joints as the knights kicked feebly, imprisoned in sixty pounds of steel.

Trained all his life for battle, the 15th century knight could fight easily on foot in 60lbs of steel plate, using sword, mace, axe or pole-arm. The well-distributed weight of armour, often exaggerated today, probably only hindered men when they fell over. Some close-visored helmets had fatally limited vision if a knight was surrounded by several enemies, however. This is Sir Edmund de Thorpe, of Norfolk, who was killed three years after Agincourt.

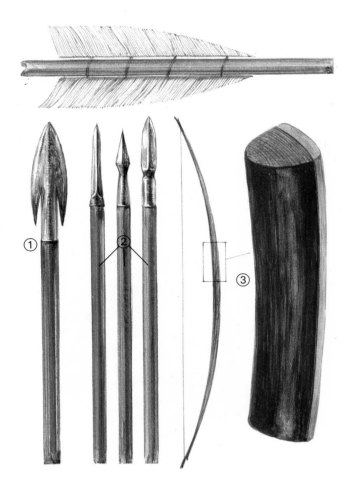

Cheap, simple bows and arrows were made in great numbers: at least 20,000 bows, 850,000 arrows in one year. One law required six feathers from each goose killed to be handed in for arrow fletching. **1** Commonest medieval arrowhead. **2** Bodkin heads; clever forging gave a hardened tip to pierce armour and a softer shank stopped shattering on impact. **3** The best bows were cut from a yew trunk with springy outer sapwood for the 'back', and compressible heartwood for the 'belly' of the bow. 300 yards' range was possible with bows of up to 120 lbs pull-weight—i.e. each pull required the same effort as lifting a sack of coal with extended arms.

In the next two hours Seth passed from a determination to sell his life dear, through amazed hope to the savage joy of victory. The huge battalions of French dismounted knights tramped slowly forward through the mud, their ranks broken and disordered by the fleeing horses of the cavalry. Their very numbers became their undoing. Disdaining the archers, they split into three great columns to attack the three little groups of English knights awaiting them lance in hand. But the narrowness of the slope, the blind pushing of the thousands of armoured men behind, and the arrows—and later the axes and clubs—of the archers on their flanks so compressed the columns that only a few dozen at the front of each had room to swing their weapons. As the English men-at-arms stabbed and slashed at those front ranks a jumbled line of dead and wounded built up along the front of the columns, over which the next ranks stumbled, pushed on by the growing pressure behind them. Cramped and half-blinded, the nobility of France became cattle for the slaughter.

For an unarmoured archer to face a knight in complete steel with only hand-to-hand weapons should have been suicide, but at the crisis of the battle Seth and his comrades did just that. Emboldened by the discovery of how helpless a knight could be if surrounded by half-a-dozen nimble killers, they had thrown down their bows when their arrows ran out, and had hurled themselves into the battle on the enemy flanks. And before the disordered crowd of Frenchmen had finally begun to falter and stumble back towards their camp, Seth and John managed to cripple one with a stab behind the knee, and had taken him prisoner as he lay helpless. Seth had been going to finish him when they wrestled his helmet off, but John had stopped the blow with an oath:

'Ar't *mad*, boy? See the gilding on this lobster's shell? See the jewels in his belt? This is some great lord's son, Seth—he's worth a shower of gold to us, boy! Take his right gauntlet—'tis the accustomed token. We'll take him to Sir Richard when we've liberty. He'll deal fair with us . . . Fie now, young fighting-cock! Lie *still*, will't thou? Thee's worth a cott, and a cow, and a feather-bed to me—aye, and a miller's daughter to lie in it, too! I'd not have thee sweat off so much as a penny-worth before I get thee to market!'

By early afternoon it was all over. The French heralds acknowledged King Henry's amazing victory, and the king gave thanks to God for a miracle. For three hours the dazed victors searched the field, stripping the dead, and either killing or taking prisoner the wounded, depending on their potential for ransom. Some of the prisoners taken early in the battle had been killed out of hand when a crisis threatened, much to the fury of their captors, but the lordling pinioned by Seth and John had survived, to their great relief. Their captain, Sir Richard de Kyghley, did not. He was one of the few English knights to die at Agincourt, and in all only a few hundred soldiers fell, against at least 7,000 Frenchmen—nearly all noblemen—and another 2,000 taken captive.

Of Sir Richard's five personal men-at-arms and eighteen archers, one died at Harfleur, two went home sick, and four died with their lord at Agincourt. Of the fifty archers from the towns around Sir Richard's estates at Inskip in Lancashire who were placed under his command for the campaign, six died at Harfleur, ten went home sick, eight were left in garrison at the port, and seven were taken prisoner in a skirmish on the march to Agincourt. The other nineteen fought and survived the battle, and returned safe to England—among them Seth and John, from the village of Tildesley south of Bolton. Unlike the other characters in this book, who have been invented as 'composites' from what history records of several men of their day, the archers of Agincourt mentioned here were real men: the record of Sir Richard de Kyghley's company still exists.

The Goddamn and his Crooked Stick

For a hundred years the English longbowman—known to his French enemy by the sneering nickname above—was the most formidable footsoldier in Europe. As long as the enemy persisted in ignoring his special strengths, and attacked him head-on over ground of his own choosing, he was almost invincible. Eventually, of course, the French stopped making it easy for him. They learned to avoid pitched battles, and patiently reconquered their ravaged country by besieging castles one by one. But the glory won by the bowmen of Crécy, Poitiers, and Agincourt is still a cherished memory.

Seth of Tildesley and his comrades were important for more than tactical reasons. They were not unwilling levies, despised, ill-treated, and ignored. They were able to command the wages of a skilled craftsman—sixpence a day in 1415, at a time when a man could eat well for a year on twenty shillings. Good wages, and—by medieval standards—fair and considerate treatment were necessary to encourage large numbers of countrymen to undertake the constant practice necessary for mastering the skills of the war-archer. In England at least, the age of the longbowman was an important step upwards in the status of the footsoldier, who has been despised by the all-conquering horseman for centuries.

The ease with which simple, unlettered men laid low the gilded aristocracy of France in their thousands played some part in hastening the end of the feudal period. Feudalism was built on the idea that the all-powerful lords paid for their limitless privileges by protecting their peasants and townsmen in time of war. Men began to ask if their masters were capable of keeping their side of the bargain any longer—if they could not, what justified their privileges?

On the battlefield the development of tactics by which the different strengths and weaknesses of knights and archers could best be harnessed together led to the beginnings of a 'modern' attitude to warfare. In fact, it was merely a resurrection of the old Roman science of war. But it replaced the chivalric idea of war as the arena in which individual displays of splendour and courage were more important than mere victory.

While common soldiers had little hope of mercy, a knight who survived the fury of battle and surrendered was normally held for ransom, in comfort and under a well-understood code of practice. Sums were often huge; the ransoms paid for over 2,000 noble captives after Poitiers, in 1356, crippled the French exchequer for a generation and beggared many families. For the common soldier or poor knight or sergeant, hopes of capturing a rich lord for ransom were a major encouragement to warfare. In the fairly rigid medieval social system it was one of the few ways to 'get rich quick'. Men often risked defeat for their army by leaving the line to escort valuable captives to the rear.

Patriots and Mercenaries
1450-1550

During the 15th century the dominance of the armoured horseman, unchallenged for 400 years, was whittled away by new infantry weapons and tactics. The two main trends were the improvement of missile weapons—bows, and early hand-held guns—and the increasingly skilled use of massed formations of men with pole-arms such as pikes and halberds. Both types of weapon cancelled out the advantage of the horseman—the 'shock' effect of his charge. A horseman's better mobility in battle counted for little if he was unable to close with the enemy. Bows and pikes both kept him at such a distance from the vulnerable body of the enemy footsoldier that he and his horse could be killed without him ever coming close enough to use his weapons. If missile and pole weapons were used together in a trained and disciplined way, the infantry became almost invulnerable.

Leaders in the use of the massed pike formation, almost identical with the Greek phalanx, were the Swiss Cantons. This loose federation of sturdily independent hill-farming communities defended their territory against many invasions. They were so successful that they became the most feared infantry in Europe—'the new Romans'. Their system of 'calling up' and organizing their army in time of danger was sensible and democratic. Each man knew his duties, his officers, and the code of discipline. When summoned to war he reported to a muster point with his own weapon, armour, and food for several days. Armour varied widely as it depended partly on wealth. Normally those with the best armour were placed in the front few ranks of the pike formation where it was needed most. Clothes in the bright, divided colours of the different Canton banners were common, as was the white cross emblem of the Confederation.

Choosing ground where slopes, trees and rocks sheltered their backs and flanks from cavalry charges, the Swiss fought in roughly square formations—sometimes several thousand strong—armed with sixteen-foot pikes. Smaller units with sword and hal-

berd for close-quarter fighting, or crossbow and hand-gun for supporting fire, darted in and out of the shelter of the pike 'phalanx', as need or opportunity arose. The pikemen themselves were by no means a static mass, but were trained to move fast in all directions without breaking their squares. A solid 'hedgehog' of thousands of gaily-dressed, brightly-armoured pikemen must have been a splendid and terrible sight as it rolled downhill in an irresistible charge, banners flying and a deep war-cry rising from thousands of throats.

With their borders finally secure, the Swiss hired themselves out as mercenaries. Europe was riven by warfare as monarchies tried to become empires. Frequent campaigns and more sophisticated infantry tactics called for large armies of trained footsoldiers. Armies could no longer be raised by feudal levy methods among national populations. So kings hired professional generals to raise and lead mercenaries according to organized rules of war. By the early 1500s German mercenaries—*Landsknechts*—were rivalling the Swiss, and went on to surpass them.

These swaggering fighting men, who wore flamboyantly 'slashed' parti-coloured costume and extravagant plumed hats, developed the basic Swiss pike tactics. The solid formations of pikemen and halberdiers were screened by ranks of men with huge two-handed swords designed to hack through the pike-shafts of the enemy. The crossbow was growing less common than the handgun—the 'arquebus'—and large numbers of handgunners surrounded and stood with the pikemen.

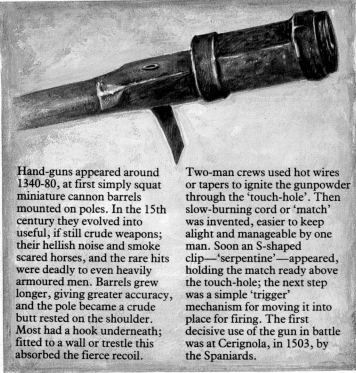

Hand-guns appeared around 1340-80, at first simply squat miniature cannon barrels mounted on poles. In the 15th century they evolved into useful, if still crude weapons; their hellish noise and smoke scared horses, and the rare hits were deadly to even heavily armoured men. Barrels grew longer, giving greater accuracy, and the pole became a crude butt rested on the shoulder. Most had a hook underneath; fitted to a wall or trestle this absorbed the fierce recoil.

Two-man crews used hot wires or tapers to ignite the gunpowder through the 'touch-hole'. Then slow-burning cord or 'match' was invented, easier to keep alight and manageable by one man. Soon an S-shaped clip—'serpentine'—appeared, holding the match ready above the touch-hole; the next step was a simple 'trigger' mechanism for moving it into place for firing. The first decisive use of the gun in battle was at Cerignola, in 1503, by the Spaniards.

Davy Hywel, Musketeer of Sir Charles Gerrard's Regiment of Foot 1645

After 150 years of supremacy, the longbow declined in importance at the beginning of the 16th century. The improving quality of handguns coincided with social factors to bring this about. Effective archer armies required large numbers of willing recruits, trained by constant practice since childhood—and they had to be strong, healthy men to use the great war-bow. In this period the English country population dropped, through famine and disease, and inflation destroyed much of the value of archers' wages. Long wars, both overseas and internal, ravaged England's military manpower. It became common to import foreign mercenaries, who used different weapons. Such men as were available at home could more quickly and easily be trained to use handguns and pikes, which needed less strength and skill. During a long peace from 1485 to 1642, few English land armies were raised, and the arts of war were largely forgotten. When civil war broke out again in that year, few of the footsoldiers had much more knowledge of fighting than Davy Hywel.

On a Saturday in June of 1645, some 10,000 Englishmen were fighting for their lives in a shallow valley outside the village of Naseby: and among them was Davy Hywel, musketeer of Sir Charles Gerrard's Bluecoats, posted in the left wing of Bard's Brigade of the Royalist army.

Davy was reloading at the rear of his regiment, and if he had not seen out of the corner of his eye the frantic waving of Lieutenant Lloyd's hat, he might have been cut down where he stood. All his attention had been on fixing the glowing slowmatch back in the cock of his musket. The din of gunfire, clash of steel, and confused roar of battle quite drowned the officer's shouts, even though he was standing only a few feet from Davy.

Following the officer's pointing arm, Davy saw long lines of steel-clad troopers looming out of the battle-smoke to his left. Now God be thanked! Prince Rupert had finally tired of chasing scattered Roundhead squadrons across the fields and was returning to aid the hard-pressed Royalist foot. Davy and his comrades had been locked 'at push of pike' with the much stronger ranks of red-coated Parliament soldiers this hour and more. The dead and dying, trampled among the muddy tussocks, marked how the battle-line had swayed back and forth. Davy had lost count of the number of times he had fired, stumbled back through the ranks to reload, and then advanced rank by rank to fire again. The measured powder charges in his rattling

bandolier of leather cartridges were long used up, and he was reloading now with loose powder from his flask, estimating the right charge by experience. He had cast the lead bullets himself, using his little portable mould; at least he could be sure they fitted his musket barrel. More than one comrade, lazier or less experienced, could be seen chewing desperately at a soft lead ball to make it fit.

Davy's head ached from the din, his fingers were sore and scorched, and the five-foot, sixteen-pound musket seemed to have doubled in weight.

But his officer was still shouting and pointing, and Davy saw to his horror that the cavalry coming up behind them from the left were not wheeling on to the flank of Lisle's Brigade—which stood on the left of Bard's, on the Royalist flank—but were charging into it. He glimpsed an officer in buff leather and black steel half-armour carrying an unfamiliar standard, and with a great orange scarf tied round his waist. Not Rupert's men, then—but Cromwell's!

Broadswords rose and fell, and horse-pistols snapped fire. Taken by surprise while their front ranks were locked in hand-to-hand combat, the green-clad formations of Lisle's musketeers and pikemen shuddered, and began to break up. The front ranks were forced back on themselves by a surge of red-coated enemy pikemen; the rear ranks tried to turn and face the threat from behind; and in the middle of the close-packed

Loading a matchlock

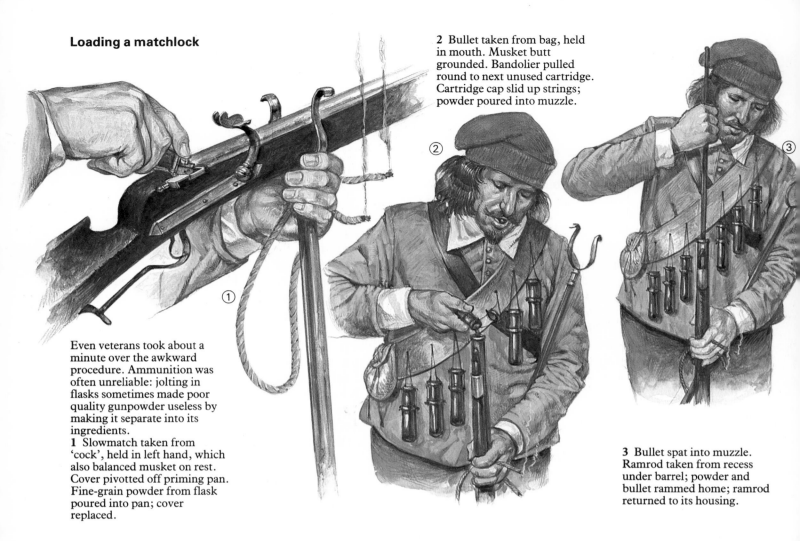

2 Bullet taken from bag, held in mouth. Musket butt grounded. Bandolier pulled round to next unused cartridge. Cartridge cap slid up strings; powder poured into muzzle.

Even veterans took about a minute over the awkward procedure. Ammunition was often unreliable: jolting in flasks sometimes made poor quality gunpowder useless by making it separate into its ingredients.
1 Slowmatch taken from 'cock', held in left hand, which also balanced musket on rest. Cover pivotted off priming pan. Fine-grain powder from flask poured into pan; cover replaced.

3 Bullet spat into muzzle. Ramrod taken from recess under barrel; powder and bullet rammed home; ramrod returned to its housing.

formation clumsy sixteen–foot pikes dipped and tangled like saplings in a storm. As Lisle's Brigade began to dissolve in panic, the first wave of cheering Parliament troopers surged up to the rear of Gerrard's Bluecoats. Davy saw hooves and swords and sinister barred visors coming straight for him.

The confusion now spread to Davy's regiment, as the rear ranks began to separate into knots of men concerned only with their own survival. Some of the musketeers were taking aim, but few pikemen had managed to order themselves, and without the shelter of their long shafts Davy felt horribly exposed.

With shaking hands he laid his musket in its forked rest; as he squinted along the barrel a horseman came charging straight at him, the heavy sword swung back for a cut at Davy's unprotected head. With a gasp of fear Davy pulled the trigger; the match dipped into the pan, there was a pink flare of burning powder—and then an agonizing pause before the stock thudded back against his bruised shoulder, and a grey-white cloud bloomed from the muzzle. The Parliament trooper disappeared in the smoke. The horse blundered past Davy, knocking the musket from his hands, and a sword went spinning through the air over his head.

There was no hope of reloading before the next wave of cavalry reached him. At that moment, after three long years, David Hywel discharged himself from the king's service. The battle was lost, and the first to run would have the best chance. Tearing off his useless bandolier, and with a pang of regret for his 'snapsack' of spare clothes and dry rations, left on the hill at the start of the battle, Davy dodged between two loose horses and ran for his life towards a sheltering spinney higher on the slope of Red Hill.

A volunteer for the King
Davy Hywel, a kitchen-maid's boy who never knew his father, had grown up in a curtained-off corner of an inn kitchen in Montgomery, a little town on the borders of England and Wales. He had worked as a pot-boy since he was old enough to push a broom, in return for the food on his platter and the straw-filled corner where he slept. His only freedom had been to run and play with his friends on Sunday afternoons, tumbling over the grassy banks of the old hill-fort above the town, or hunting for wood-blewitts and oyster-fungus in the autumn beechwoods of Ffriddfaldwyn.

News travelled slowly to an illiterate pot-boy in a

4 Musket returned to rest. Slowmatch—blown or swung until burning brightly—returned to 'cock'.

5 Pan cover pivotted off to expose priming powder. Take aim.

6 Fire! Pulling trigger swings 'cock' down, brings end of match into priming powder. This flares, and sparks pass through the touch-hole into the main charge in the barrel, setting it off after a 'hang-fire' of about a second.

remote border town; but in 1642 Davy could not help learning of a great rebellion against King Charles—the streets and tap-rooms were buzzing with it. And on a fine morning soon afterwards he heard that one Colonel Charles Gerrard, a dashing cavalier who had fought in foreign wars, had arrived in Montgomery to recruit men in the king's interest. The plumed and laced officers came into Davy's inn to drink, swearing wonderfully and propping their huge boots on the scrubbed tables. They told him that all volunteers would be provided with fine blue suits at the Colonel's expense, and with new muskets worth all of sixteen shillings, together with every necessary accoutrement. Each volunteer would be paid four whole shillings a week, and would eat the finest wheaten bread and yellow cheese, washed down with rivers of beer.

Davy had never had four shillings in coin in his life. He yearned to escape the inn kitchen, and his master's kicks and hard words. The dazzling warriors slapped his back, and called him a young hero, and showed him where to make his cross on the paper. And so Davy Hywel marched off to fight for his king, to the *tuck* of a drum and the tears of his mother and sisters, with a fine blue doublet on his back and a jay's wing stuck jauntily in his new hat.

After generations of peace the only men in England qualified to raise and lead armies were the soldiers of fortune who had fought the terrible wars which had devastated Germany and the Low Countries for the past thirty years. Gentlemen who had served under the King of Sweden or the Princes of Orange were given commissions to recruit around the country, and to try and pass on their knowledge to their rag-tag regiments. Warfare was a newly refined science, based upon a marriage of new weapons and tactics with the surviving books of the ancient Roman and Greek tacticians, whose study was now fashionable once more among educated men. The theories were complicated. Manuals of arms illustrated thirty or forty different drill movements for pikemen and musketeers. The ordering of armies in the field could involve complex formations and movements designed to serve any situation. In practice, things were a lot simpler.

Davy lacked the strength to handle the huge pikes with which half the regiment was still armed. But the matchlock musket required little strength, and like most boys who had spent years throwing stones, Davy had a good enough 'eye' to learn to shoot a musket fairly easily. Cumbersome, much slower, and of shorter range than the bow of old, the musket was still 'the great equalizer'. Under the instruction of his officers, Captain Windebanke and Lieutenant Euble Lloyd, Davy soon picked up the minimum of skill to make him a potentially deadly enemy to men much stronger and more experienced than himself.

The regiment's 500 or so musketeers were drawn up for battle in two eight-rank blocks, one on each side of a central block of about 500 pikemen. The pikes could protect the musketeers from sudden charges by enemy horse or foot at awkward moments—the reloading process took minutes at a time, and in high wind or rain the musketeers might be left helpless. If all went well, repeated volleys of musketry delivered by ranks of men firing and falling back to reload in turn could do terrible execution on close-packed regiments of enemies up to about fifty yards range. Thus weakened, they could be swept away by a charge with levelled pikes.

Most of the actions in which Davy fought were simple head-on clashes between two long lines of infantry regiments grouped two or three together into brigades. The cavalry were usually drawn up on the flanks of the battle-line, and fought each other. Their half-armour, swords and pistols were no match for the massed pikes and heavy bullets of a steady infantry brigade of two or three thousand men. In the best-drilled units the musketeers learned how to side-step into the open spaces between the files of pikes when threatened by cavalry; in this refuge they could fire and reload in complete safety. But if infantry were caught from the flank or rear, or strung out in the open, it was a bloodier affair altogether—particularly if their opponents were the well-trained troopers of Parliament's New Model Army.

Davy's first enthusiasm did not last many months. In the early days of his service he was carried away by the excitement of new experiences, by the splendid show of flags and clothes and drums. But as the king's army marched around central England, in counties of which Davy had never heard and among folk whose accents he could not understand, he stopped feeling like the hero of some old ballad and grew homesick for familiar things. Many men around him deserted. They risked hanging, to slip away and return to families and harvests which needed them. Pay seldom appeared on time, if at all. Often soldiers went hungry, ragged, and footsore, for their commanders lacked the organization to see their men properly provisioned. The ranks dwindled, and were filled up again with unwilling civilians kidnapped from plough or cottage as the hungry army straggled by. Enemy prisoners were sometimes forced to change sides at the sword's point. Keeping such an army together took harsh discipline. The dozens of 'laws and ordinances of war' read out to Davy's regiment at each parade all seemed to end with the depressing words '. . . upon pain of death without mercy'.

There was death in plenty, and not only from enemy steel and shot. Disease raged through the dirty camps and wet bivouacs, and there were few doctors with the time to care for common soldiers. Accidents killed and maimed several of Davy's comrades. With men whirling lengths of burning slowmatch round their heads to keep them alight, and barrels of loose gunpowder everywhere, there were often hideous mishaps.

When Davy finally crept out of his spinney on the night after Naseby he intended to search for his discarded kitbag. But the sight of thousands of dead and dying lying crumpled in the moonlight, and the lanterns of enemy soldiers searching for friends and stripping the dead, and the terrible sounds he heard in the dark all overcame his courage. In the days which followed he tried to find his way back to Montgomery. He knew he had to go westwards, but apart from that he had no idea where he was. The muddy roads were few, and the names on the occasional milestones were no help to a man who could not read. The villages were poor clusters of cottages, plundered already by so many soldiers of both sides that at sight of a stranger they barred their doors and loosed the dogs. Roundhead patrols jingled along the lanes, and the sight of the murdered women and camp-servants in the Royalist lines after Naseby had shown Davy what mercy he could expect if they spotted him.

Nuts and berries grubbed from hedgerows as he wandered by night were not enough to sustain Davy's strength. Wet ditches made unhealthy beds as he hid by day. Not long passed before he was wracked with chills. All one night he lay shivering in the dew, too ill to search for food, and thus he grew even weaker. By the following night he could not move: chills had turned to fever. His head ached, his joints were stiff and swollen, and his mind began to play tricks on him. As he slid into delirium his last clear thought was a pang of sadness for his mother and sisters. They had heard no word from him these past three years.

Development of regimental uniforms, 1680s–1750s

These are British examples; most armies followed broadly similar trends. **1** *Musketeer, Hastings' Regt., 1689.* 'Slouch' hat of 1640s now more formal, trimmed with ribbon, and brim cocked. Red coat of 1640s' New Model Army retained, though cut follows civilian style of day. Coloured 'facings', chosen by the colonel and not yet centrally regulated, distinguished each regiment. These were the last years of the 'Twelve Apostles' bandolier and the first of the 'plug' bayonet, jammed in gun muzzle for close combat. The musket is an early flintlock—see p.45.

2 *Grenadier, 1704.* Hand grenades, with fuze lit by slowmatch, were now used in some assaults by the strongest, most daring men forming a 'Grenadier Company' in each regiment. To make throwing more practical, the wide hat was replaced by a cap, and the musket fitted with a sling. Cartridges and grenades were carried in pouches. All soldiers carried swords. The 'socket' bayonet, fitting outside the muzzle, allowed firing while fitted. Élite soldiers —grenadiers, Royal guards, drummers, etc.—now wear tape loops as coat decoration. Canvas gaiters with straps under the foot prevented shoes coming off in mud.

3 *'Sentinel of Foot', 1704.* Private of non-grenadier company now has a hat cocked up on three sides.

4 *Corporal, 45th Foot, 1750.* The coat has become formalized and decorative; regulations govern regimental 'facing', lace pattern, etc. The hat is a fully-cocked tricorn. The shoulder-knot indicates an NCO. 'Grenadiers' were still the élite company of each unit, although grenades were no longer used.

5 *Grenadier, Conway's Regt., 1746.* Simple cap is now a stiff, regulation 'mitre' with Royal badge. Grenadiers still have decorative brass match-case on cross-belt and are further distinguished by laced 'wings' on coat shoulders.

NEC ASPERA TERRENT

Musketeer Jochen Reiner of Infantry Regiment No. 18 'Prince of Prussia' 1748

The English Parliament's New Model Army, which defeated King Charles at Naseby, was the first English example of a type of army which appeared in many European countries during the 17th century. For the first time since the days of Rome, these were paid, trained, professional 'standing armies', which served in peacetime as well as in time of national emergency. The last echo of the old feudal days was silenced, as kings brought power into the hands of their central governments. The 18th century brought increasing wealth from trade, making it possible to pay full-time troops. In war they were the instrument of their government; in peacetime, they too often became elaborately-dressed 'toys' for monarchs to parade around according to ever-more complex manuals of drill. One army which glittered like toy soldiers on parade, but which also triumphed in many battles, was the Prussian army of the mid-18th century, brought to a peak of efficiency by the soldier-king Frederick the Great. We may imagine the life of a typical Prussian musketeer, during an interlude of peace.

'Idiot! Idle lout!' *Crack* came Lieutenant Zohndorf's cane across the ear of the unfortunate soldier beside Jochen in the ranks. As Jochen braced himself rigidly to

attention, being careful not to draw the officer's furious scowl upon himself by so much as a quiver, he reflected that poor old Franz would be more worried about the state of his hat, now lying in the muddy grass, than about his bruised face.

With only ten days to go until the spring review the men of Infantry Regiment No. 18 'Prince of Prussia', were spending every available hour on the practice ground, and their uniforms had to be as perfect as their marching. If Franz's hat had got muddy he would be spending this evening carefully drying and brushing it, instead of coming down to the inn with Jochen. Officers didn't care about such things, of course, with servants to keep their uniforms spotless.

Not that he blamed the lieutenant. It was rumoured that he was in bad favour anyway, and naturally he was nervous about putting his men through their paces under the merciless eye of Old Fritz himself. King Frederick had been known to ruin the careers of his officers as casually as the officers hit their men. Blows and curses were all part of a musketeer's life, after all, and Jochen had to admit that Franz's drill had lost some of its 'snap' during the past six months' winter leave at home.

Apart from these tense weeks around the regiment's Spandau depot when spring and autumn exercises were looming, Jochen had little fault to find with a

Prussian soldier's life. At least it was simple. All he had to do was keep his kit clean, and obey his sergeants and officers instantly and without question. Nobody expected him to think things out for himself, and he found that restful. He got a bit confused when he didn't have routine to guide him. He had a cosy billet, good comrades, and usually enough pocket-money for beer and tobacco. In times of peace, he could go home to his father's farm on leave for nearly ten months of the year!

Real Prussians were not expected to report for duty at the headquarters of the regiment except for a matter of weeks twice a year, for the spring and autumn inspections. The foreign mercenaries who made up more than half of the regiment were quite enough for peacetime duties. And then again, while the native-born soldiers were on leave, the company captain could keep their pay and allowances for himself! Jochen had heard that Captain von Auerbach had made more than 3,000 dollars last year—an unimaginable fortune. Jochen would have to soldier for . . . well, at two dollars a month, that made twenty-four a year, so divide 3,000 by—well, he gave up, figuring was never his strong point, but it was a devilish long time, away. Even Lieutenant Zohndorf only got thirteen dollars a month: no wonder he was so anxious to make a good impression on the king, and get promoted to company commander himself!

As the third son of a small farmer, without a trade, business or inheritance to qualify him for exemption from military service, Jochen was singled out while still a boy for the region's quota of conscripts. In due course he found himself in a blue and white uniform faced with the smart pink of the 18th Infantry, holding a corner of a tattered banner in the garrison church and stumbling over the oath which the adjutant dictated. They gave him a silver coin, a receipt (which he couldn't read) for his uniform, and there he was: a conscripted Prussian soldier, until death, crippling wounds or infirmity released him to the grave or a poverty-stricken old age. There was no point in worrying about that now. He had plenty of more immediate worries in this strange new life. Life on the farm had been getting a bit uncomfortable. It was a tiny place, and with his four sisters and two brothers there wasn't much room, or food. Nobody took much notice of Jochen, at home or in the village. But to wear King Frederick's coat, well, that would make certain people pay him a bit more attention! Mark you, there were terrible stories about the way soldiers were treated . . . but his father and big brothers had been none too gentle with him, and people usually stretched the truth a bit, anyway.

He had been sent with six other men to a 'billet' in a tailor's house in the town—a couple of rooms in the attics. The army paid for them as there were not nearly enough proper barracks to house all the soldiers. There they slept, and cooked their food, and mended and cleaned their uniforms, and generally lived a fairly pleasant life when they were off duty.

An old soldier was ordered to take charge of them

and see that they didn't make life too boisterous for the tailor and his family. The same old veteran was told to keep a special eye on Jochen—to show him how to look after his kit, how to dress his own and his comrades' hair in a long, tight pigtail with curls over the ears, how to salute the remote and God-like officers, how to avoid the wrath of brutal sergeants, and how to get his fair share of bed-straw, food, and space at the fire on winter nights. Like all new recruits he got ragged a bit at first but after a few scuffles he was accepted as a good comrade.

For his first year he served full time at the depot in Spandau. All he had to learn was the drill manual—but that was quite enough, especially as he couldn't read and had to be shown everything over and over again. There seemed to be a thousand orders, and he had to learn to interpret these strange shouts, and snap into the right position like an iron puppet.

To start with the officers and sergeants were quite patient, taking recruits off by themselves in twos and threes and going over the movements slowly. But after six months Musketeer Reiner was posted to a proper unit—the 1st Company of the 2nd Battalion—and being a fine big lad he was put in the front rank, where everyone could see him. From then onwards he was expected to be perfect in his drill, and if he made a mistake there were plenty of fists and canes to point it out to him.

Even so, Jochen was not unhappy. He enjoyed the rough comradeship of his mates, in their smokey little rooms over the tailor's shop. He soon found out that a soldier could have plenty of spare time, and nobody nagged at him when he was off duty. Often he was allowed to take part-time jobs with local tradesmen, loading carts or stacking barrels, to make a bit more pocket money—after the usual stoppages for uniform and food, there wasn't much left of his six pennies a day wages. The respect the civilians showed for the king's soldiers made his chest swell with pride, and he walked the streets with a swagger. After the life of a farm-boy, the inns in the backstreets of Spandau were a real eye-opener, too. He was soon swigging beer and schnapps, and puffing on a clay pipe, and exchanging jokes with the serving girls, just like his comrades. He got into a few scrapes before he learned how to cope with this new life, of course. Once, horribly drunk and with stains on his waistcoat, he was late for Sunday church parade. That cost him an afternoon of agony astride the 'wooden horse'—a sharp trestle affair made out of a sawing-horse, which hurt so much he could hardly walk afterwards. But he never got into real trouble, and took care not to—the penalties were too terrifying, even for a rough country lad. Once, just before his regiment marched off to the Silesian War, he saw one of the French mercenaries in his company punished for his part in a mass-desertion plot. The poor

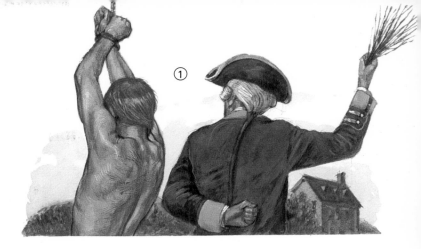

18th and 19th–century soldiers were often 'hard cases', but the extreme brutality of the punishments they suffered for even minor crimes hardly made them better soldiers. At best it produced machine-like obedience from men more frightened of their officers than of the risk of death in battle—which was believed to be a desirable attitude, well into the 19th century. The Prussian army was particularly harsh; common methods were **1** flogging, with up to 1,500 lashes being inflicted over several hours; death under the lash was not uncommon. Less dangerous but still agonizing were **2** the 'wooden horse', and **3** the tying of opposite limbs for hours at a time, producing agonies of cramp. A Prussian speciality was 'running the gauntlet' **4** the victim was forced repeatedly down a lane of 200 soldiers who beat him with sticks. The NCO's pike at his chest kept the pace slow. The band often played to drown his screams. Death was not unusual.

Infantry battalion formation of 18th century—here, British, about 1710, but there was little difference from nation to nation for half a century. About 800 men are in three ranks, the front kneeling, so all can fire without changing position. Officers, sergeants, and drummers stand on flanks and behind, to give and pass on orders. To keep an even fire from all parts of the line, the unit is divided into eighteen platoons in three 'firings'. At the command those platoons here shown in blue fire a volley; then those in red; then those in green, by which time the first group should have reloaded. Cannon on flanks gave support, being manhandled forward in any advance. In battle the din, the smoke and different reloading speeds of the men made such complex systems break down after two or three volleys, and firing became ragged.

devil was sentenced by the colonel to thirty-six 'runs of the gauntlet'. He died on the second day, half way through his twentieth run. Jochen would rather face cannon than run the gauntlet.

He *had* faced cannon, too: the 18th Infantry were at the battle of Kesseldorf, near Dresden, three years ago in the freezing December of 1745. Now Jochen remembered mostly the cold, and the pain of his blisters, and the miserable nights his squad spent shivering in a sodden tent in the snow, too tired and wet-through to sleep. The battle itself had been confusing, but not as frightening as he had secretly feared. He really didn't see much, so it wasn't too bad. The officers had lined the army up facing the Saxons across a frozen river, but when the cannons started firing everything was soon hidden by rolling banks of dirty-white smoke. When the drums beat the signal the 18th had started marching forward, straight towards the enemy artillery batteries. Jochen had concentrated on keeping in perfect line with his comrades, just as he had been taught—and it wasn't easy in the thick snow and ice. Every now and then he would hear the wicked howl of grape-shot through the smoke, and men would fall into the slush, staining it pink with their blood. But the ranks closed up and kept moving, so they were soon left behind. As long as you kept counting the pace in your head, and fixed your eyes ahead, it wasn't too bad. When they were close enough to see an orange glare in the smoke every time the cannons roared, they were ordered to stop and fire. Jochen primed, rammed, and fired many times, mostly just blind into the smoke, although a breath of wind shifted it once and he thought he saw a Saxon gunner fall at his shot. It wasn't his job to think about targets: it was up to the officers to lead the regiment into a position where they could do some damage. The 18th lost about 350 men out of 1,700 in that battle, he heard—the veterans said that was getting off easy.

After the battle he recalled that a Dutchman in his company said that the Prussian musket wasn't as good as foreign ones. He said the walnut stock was too weak, and could break at the thin neck if you slammed it down during drill, and that it was too muzzle-heavy, sending most of the shots into the ground at the enemy's feet. Jochen didn't know if it was true, but what did foreigners know, anyway? The Prussians were the best soldiers on earth, everyone knew that. Brandenburgers like the 18th Infantry were the best Prussians of all! With Old Fritz to lead them, they could capture Hell itself.

At last even Lieutenant Zohndorf had had enough for one day, and the battalion was dismissed. As he walked back to his billet Jochen was trying to calculate how many hours it would take to clean and polish his uniform and kit for tomorrow, and if he had time to stroll down to the Black Stag. Johanna, the cook, had a twinkling eye for a fine strapping musketeer; and with Franz out of the way he would have no rival for her attentions! The way she did diced pork and swedes more than made up for her squint and the gaps in her teeth . . . All in all, not a bad life.

The flintlock musket

The weapon of the world's infantry from about 1670 to 1840, the flintlock, underwent few substantial changes in that time. Its advantages were lightness, allowing it to be aimed without a rest, and the self-contained firing system which did away with dangerous burning matches, and allowed use in most weathers. The jaws of the 'cock' held a flint wedge which dropped onto an angled steel plate, the 'frizzen', producing sparks. The frizzen doubled as a spring-loaded cover for the priming pan, protecting the powder from wind and rain until the moment of firing. Almost simultaneously with the flintlock, self-contained ammunition was invented. The main powder charge and ball were wrapped together in a paper tube, which could be mass-produced and issued in quantity. Tactics now became more sophisticated in one sense, since large units could count on firing often, reliably and together, on command. The pike was no longer needed to fend off cavalry, and was discarded. But the short accurate range still limited tactics to close-up confrontations between tight-packed formations of men. A Prussian general tested an élite unit's marksmanship with flintlocks against a target 10 feet high and 30 feet wide. At 150 yards only 46 out of 100 balls hit it at all; at 200 yards, only 17. Even trained men took half a minute to load. In the heat of battle many men rammed in more than one cartridge without firing at all, causing jamming or disastrous explosions. Others used early wooden ramrods too roughly and broke them, leaving themselves unable to load again. Surprisingly many accounts mention soldiers firing away their ramrods—firing with the ramrod still in the barrel. Even without such mishaps muskets needed constant care. Flints became chipped, shifting in the jaws of the cock, and needed adjustment or replacement after a dozen or so shots. Burnt powder quickly fouled and clogged touch-hole and barrel, and soldiers carried wire brushes and 'bodkins' to keep the mechanism clean.

The frizzen is in open position, the flint is back in 'half-cock' safety position. Paper cartridge taken from pouch.

The folded-over end of the cartridge is bitten off.

Some powder is poured into the priming pan, covering the touch-hole which connects with the base of the barrel. The spring-loaded frizzen is clicked back to retain and protect the priming.

Remaining powder is poured down barrel; the ball—with paper still attached, making a wad to hold powder and ball tightly in place—is pushed down after it.

The ramrod, taken from the 'pipes' under the barrel, is used to thump the ball well home on top of the powder, and is then replaced.

The flint is clicked back to 'full-cock' position; the musket is ready to fire, and the soldier takes rough aim along the barrel.

Pulling the trigger releases the spring-loaded cock; it falls, and the flint hits the frizzen, knocking it up and forward, while the sparks of the impact fall into the exposed priming powder.
The priming flares in a slow explosion; sparks travel through the touch-hole to the main charge and set it off, after a 'hang fire' of about a second— enough for the soldier to flinch at the flaring powder in front of his eyes, and ruin his aim.

Private Pharoah Kyte, His Majesty's 44th Regiment of Foot
1815

In its rigid conservatism the late 18th-century army began dangerously to resemble a sort of cumbrous military dinosaur— so heavy with blind obedience to old methods that it was unable to react to new circumstances. The static pattern was broken in the 1790s, when the eager, untrained patriot armies of Revolutionary France inflicted defeat after defeat on armies of the old school. During the Napoleonic Wars, a new breed of imaginative commanders—men like Sir John Moore, Lord Wellington, and above all, Napoleon himself—married the best of the old disciplines with a new, practical, professional approach. They brought the skills of 'black powder' warfare to a new peak of effectiveness. Their soldiers, both conscripts and volunteers, still came from the poorest class of society; and though they covered themselves with glory in battle, their life was still terribly hard, and their rewards pitiful. A reminder of this might have been heard on a London street corner, perhaps, some day during the 1850s:

'Spare a copper, mate? Spare a copper for an old soldier-man, lady? Spare a shilling, Your Honour —a shilling, for a Waterloo man?. . . A *sovereign!* Well, good luck and health to you, sir, for a proper gent!

'Aye, Your Honour, it's true enough—here's my medal to prove it, with my name struck in, see? Pharoah Kyte by name, sir, rear rank man in Captain Pearce's company of the 44th of Foot—the East Essex Regiment, what took the Frenchy eagle-flag at Salamanca. Oh yes, Your Honour, I was there too—three year in the Peninsula, and then Waterloo, Sunday the eighteenth of June, 1815—and my leg's there still, for all I know! But they give me the medal to prove I were there. First medal they ever give to common soldier-men, it was.

'You'd be a military gent yourself, sir? Foot Guards, I dare say? Just so, just so—you can't mistake the set of a man who's worn King George's coat . . . Why, thank'ee kindly, Captain—be proud to take a quart with you! There's an honest tap just by here, where you'll meet no disrespect . . . Your health, Captain—here's to a bloody war and quick promotion! . . . And here's another to the Great Duke, God rest his soldier's bones!

'No, Captain, it would be pitching it high to say we ever *loved* old Hooky—he didn't set out for to be loved, you see. But we *trusted* him, and that's worth a deal more. We knew he'd not toss our lives away without need . . . Kept us to our duty, did Hooky, officers and men alike, and none harder than his own self. But he knew what a man could do, and what he plain couldn't, and he ordered us according. He knew we had to shift as best we could when we was campaigning in them

foreign parts. Long as we had sixty cartridges in our pouch, and we was *where* he said, *when* he said—why, *he* never cared how we looked!

'Like gypsies, sir, mostly, since you ask. You may think this old red coat a sad sort of an article now, but you should have seen your own Foot Guards after a season in them Spanish hills! Patched all over like a scabby dog, and not a pair of boots between each file! There was days you could follow us by the bloody footprints on the stones, Captain—and by the poor souls whose mates couldn't drag 'em along any further, and dropped behind, and got sliced up like a porker's cheek by Boney's dragoons . . . Your boots is your best friend, Captain, better nor Brown Bess herself. If your boots break down, your feet soon look like a man's back after 500 lashes, and you drop behind on the march. Lose your battalion, and you're done for, out in them foreign parts.

'Look at them young peacocks over there, sir, coming it the high horse around the town! *That's* not soldiering. How many of them ever seen a good comrade die in his tracks of the sun and the weight of his knapsack? How many of them could fight Boney's grenadiers after sleeping all night in the mud? Lord bless you, Captain, we didn't have no *tents* in them days! Just a poor thin greatcoat, and a blanket like a sodden dish-cloth—and billhooks, to cut branches for a little kind of a shelter, like, if so happened there was any to cut! If there wasn't, we slept on God's bare earth, and a damned cold couch she makes, too. Mornings, the blanket'd be frozen hard to the mud . . .

'Always seemed to be some kind of alarm just when we was cooking our grub, too. The beeves marched with us, see, and at night they'd butcher a few. You'd get a chunk, all raw and hairy, and mostly muscle; and set it to boil in a kettle, or spit it on a ramrod over the embers while you pounded your biscuit. We used to grind it up with water in a kind of a porridgey mess, 'stirabout' we called it—only way to eat the biscuit, it were that hard. Then damn me if the drums wouldn't beat! "To arms!", and off we'd march—pots overset on the fires, and men stuffing bits of three-parts-raw meat in their haversacks, all covered in ash and dirt, to chew on the march.

'Why'd I enlist? To fill my belly, Captain, same as most. I was a cowman over to Colchester, see; and there was a bit of bother over a girl, and I lost my place, and my character in the parish. So when the recruiting party comes round the villages, beating the drums for volunteers for the Regulars, I took the shilling. The bounty were £25—a great sum to me, sir. Mark you, that recruiting sergeant helped me spend most of it that night in the Pied Bull! So that's how I came to the Peninsular Field Army, Lord Wellington commanding—and to France and Belgium after.

'Aye, sir, a damned rough lot—but it was a

Pharoah Kyte's equipment

on campaign could weigh up to 60lbs; the listed items were a normal minimum, in addition to which he took turns to carry squad cooking pots, camping tools, etc. **1** Shako, with rain-flap; it replaced the old cocked hat in 1800. **2** Hair was not pigtailed or powdered after 1808. **3** Rolled greatcoat and blanket—8lbs. **4** Of tarred cloth and leather, with a painfully uncomfortable wooden frame and chest-strap which crushed the lungs dangerously, the 'Trotter' knapsack held: 2 prs.shoes, 2 prs. stockings, 1 pr. gaiters, 2 shirts, 1 pr. trousers, 1 fatigue jacket and cap, 4 brushes, buttonstick, comb, pipeclay for cleaning belts, pen, ink, paper, personal belongings—about 18lbs. **5** Mess-dish. **6** Wooden water-bottle—full, about 4lbs. **7** Haversack with three days' bread, two days' beef—5lbs. **8** Socket bayonet, 1ft 5 ins long—1lb. **9** Pouch, 60 ball cartridges—6lbs. **10** Uniform now more practical; single-breasted jacket with regimentally-coloured 'facings' and lace, and false, short-cut 'turn-backs' at tail. Loose campaign trousers made from any local cloth. **11** 'Brown Bess', the strong, simple, reliable India Pattern smooth bore musket of ·753 calibre, 4ft 11ins long without bayonet—9lb 11oz.

Cannon-shot, sabres and lances did dreadful damage. Even musket balls, huge and slow compared with today's bullets, made massive splintered wounds rather than neat holes. Surgeons had no knowledge of germs, or even of the importance of cleanliness. They knew serious wounds usually became infected, so were quick to amputate wounded limbs. With no anaesthetic apart from a stiff drink, patients were often amazingly stoic, but the pain of long operations killed many from shock, so surgeons practised very fast amputations. The stump was often cauterised with hot tar. About one amputee in four died. Even so, there are records of many extraordinary recoveries, including several men who survived between ten and twenty wounds in one battle. Disease, and infection after the operation itself, killed far more men than outright wounds.

damned hard duty, and no lady's maids watching how we did it, neither. But good comrades all—fine men to stand beside you in a fight. Best army old England ever sent over seas, they do still say. Mark you, the Frenchies could fight—no mistake about that. But they was wicked cruel, too—you'd not believe some of the things we saw in Spain. Not that I took much to the Spanishers neither, come to that. Lot of gabbling Papists, torturing prisoners, eating all kinds of muck cooked in lamp-oil, and pull a knife soon as look at you!

'Well, no, Badajoz was a bad business, sir, no denying that. We could be cruel too, when the madness was on us. But fair's fair, Captain—Badajoz was fear, and fighting hand-to-hand all night, and seeing too many good comrades die, and then the liquor on top of all. We stopped being soldiers and turned into devils, once we was through the walls . . . No mending it now.

'Waterloo, sir? Well, I'll not stretch a tale for a military gent, it were just like all the rest, only more so, if you take my meaning. We marched all day in the rain, and we slept all night in the mud, and we fought Boney all next day. Seemed to go on for ever, it did. Never did I hear so many cannon in my life, fair deafening it were. I can't rightly remember much about particular doings, sir. I saw Sir Thomas Picton die, him in his old top hat, mouth open on a curse, like always. That was when he led us forward—the 44th, and the Black Watch and

Gordons, and "Pontius Pilate's Bodyguard", all good old Peninsula corps. We put some poor raggedy French infantry to the rightabouts, I remember. Then we just stood in squares, watching the Frenchy cavalry, while them cannon just tore at us, and tore at us . . . Did you know, Captain, in them days you could *see* a cannon-ball flying at you if it came straight?

'Yes, I seen the one what did for me, all black against the white smoke. Then the head came off poor George Byfield in front of me, and the earth threw me like a horse, and I looked down and seen what they done to me . . . The bandsmen carried me to the surgeon in the rear, where he was cutting up a lot of other poor souls, and they give me as much gin as I could swallow. Surgeon takes one look, and "Up on the chests with him, lads", he says, "hold him down . . ."

'So that were the end of my soldiering, Captain. Nigh on forty year ago, now . . . Mind, I've been luckier than most. I went before the Board of Commissioners at Chelsea, and they give me a ticket for sixpence a day as an out-pensioner. And I got my licence to beg, from the Justices. I can still do odd bits of this and that for my keep. Gents like you still stop for the Waterloo Medal, now and then.

'But it ain't much for your youth, and strength, and one of your legs, is it, Your Honour? Sixpence a day? It ain't much . . .'

Move and Counter-move

The armies of the Napoleonic Wars were generally made up of the same types of troops, units and weapons as those of the 18th century. The new factor was leadership. Napoleon himself, one of the greatest military geniuses of history, won an extraordinary series of victories by clear strategy and audacious tac-

The classic 'Napoleonic' attack, in phases:

1 Massed French cannon fire a long barrage on unimaginatively drawn-up enemy in line formation, thinning their ranks and shaking their morale. Forbidden to move to take cover, the infantry lose many men—round-shot and explosive shells could kill half-a-dozen at a time.

2 Strong units of French sharpshooters work their way close to the enemy line under cover of terrain, and kill many more of them by sniping with muskets. Light artillery were often brought forward to support them, guarded by cavalry, once they had taken control of the ground between the main battle-lines.

3 Massed columns of French infantry move forward against weak points of the enemy line, breaking into a charge when within range. Although column formation allowed few to use their muskets, the enemy's fire was by now usually too weak and unco-ordinated to prevent the columns breaking through their formation.

4 Strong cavalry forces are sent in to exploit gaps in enemy lines, cutting the enemy army into groups and working outwards, taking those units still resisting from flank or rear. Once the enemy were dispersed they were lost; cavalry would pursue them, turning defeat into hopeless rout, as much by the psychological effect of cavalry charges as by actual sword-cuts.

tics. Most of the nations ranged in arms against him produced in response one or two leaders who 'on a good day' could beat the French—or at least avoid defeat. On the battlefield the issue was usually decided in favour of the general who manipulated most intelligently the strengths and weaknesses of the different 'arms'—horse, foot, and guns. Morale, training, and choice of time and ground were vital, but the basic tactics may be seen as a deadly version of the children's game of Scissors, Paper, and Stone. Under one set of circumstances the cavalry could sweep away the infantry; under another, the infantry could break the cavalry . . .

The classic 'Wellingtonian' defence against each phase:

1 Infantry drawn up behind a crest–even a slight fold of ground gave good protection against artillery. Men were often ordered to lie down in ranks, to cut the size of the target further. Most artillery shot passed overhead, hit ground in front and bounced over, or burst there harmlessly.

2 French skirmishers are met, and beaten at their own game, by even stronger forces of light infantry, including green–clad riflemen with weapons which outranged muskets. Defenders win control of 'No Man's Land'; keep enemy horse artillery at bay; and snipe at the main attack as it advances.

3 Moving forward at the last moment, the infantry line is still strong and unshaken. Much greater numbers of defenders' muskets can be brought to bear than those in the cramped enemy columns. Fired on from three directions, these were often driven off with heavy losses.

4 If unbroken infantry have even slight warning of the enemy cavalry attack they can adopt square formation, almost invulnerable to cavalry; horses will not charge home against massed bayonets and volley-fire. *But* squares are very vulnerable to artillery, and can be smashed by guns if forced to hold this formation by clever cavalry manoeuvres nearby.

Private Wilkes of Company K, 20th Maine Volunteers, 1863

By the mid-19th century it was slowly being accepted—in some armies, painfully slowly—that the common soldier was owed better treatment than Pharoah Kyte received. In America this movement towards reform of medical services, military justice, and the provision of clothing and equipment which was practical as well as smart was encouraged by the Civil War of the 1860s. It was obviously unacceptable to treat free men who volunteered out of personal conviction in the same way that older armies treated men who enlisted from hunger. But the physical suffering of the soldier on campaign was, if anything, worse—for the rapid growth of industry and technology put him into battle in the same massed formations as Napoleon's soldiers, but now faced by weapons of greater destructive power and accuracy. This war saw the first major use of repeating rifles, accurate breech-loading artillery, telescopic sights, crude machine guns, troop movement by railway, and communications by telegraph.

Last summer Jonathan Minshul Wilkes, a doctor's son from Portland, Maine, was gazing out of a lecture-hall window at Bowdoin College, wishing he could be sailing his skiff instead of listening to Professor Lawrence Chamberlain's explanation of Greek rhetoric.

On this muggy evening, the second of July 1863, Private Wilkes of Company K, 20th Maine Volunteers, sits on a rough stone parapet on a hill in Pennsylvania, swilling water round a mouth dried by fear and by biting open black-powder cartridges. He is 17 years old. He has just fought for his life, and for this vital position on Little Round Top at the very end of the Union Army's line at Gettysburg, against a desperate Confederate attack—and he fought under command of Colonel Lawrence Chamberlain.

Jonathan's brother, George, and several classmates also serve in his former teacher's regiment. Most of the officers and men have known each other's families all their lives. This makes the rigid discipline of professional soldiers impossible; but it gives these half-trained civilians in uniform a valuable feeling of 'family' and security which is good for morale.

Jonathan is a soldier of conscience, like most men fighting in this American Civil War. He did not enlist for pay, nor to serve a remote government power as a professional fighting man. He volunteered, for this war only, in defence of a political principle. His father voted for President Lincoln. The attempt by the southern states to split the nation and form their independent 'Confederacy' has been hotly discussed in the Wilkes home. This evening some 500 Maine soldiers defended Lincoln's policy among these boulders and trees, and about 140 of them have suffered death or wounds in the process.

Jonathan's father calls the Southern politicians 'slaveocrats'—slave-owning tyrants, unfit for power in a modern democracy. But the ragged Alabama farmboys who came boiling up the hill out of the dark woods

this evening, howling their terrible wolfish battle-yell, didn't look as if they owned many slaves. Some didn't even own shoes. The 'Rebs' are hungry, threadbare, short of every military resource—but their courage is legendary, and they have beaten the Union Army time and again. So Jonathan reckons they must be fighting for a principle too. It is all very confusing; but his mind is still too full of the fear and savagery of the fight to puzzle it out now.

It had been a desperately close thing. The 20th Maine were very nearly overrun; when their cartridges ran out they only saved the hill by following Colonel Chamberlain in a frantic bayonet charge. Soldiers in this war rarely kill each other with bayonets. The cruel steel spike is more commonly used as a toasting-fork and entrenching tool than a weapon. Today Jonathan saw a man die on a bayonet for the first time, and hated it.

Training and fighting

This was not Jonathan's first battle, but his preparation for it has been hasty and sketchy. The Union Army has increased from fewer than 20,000 to half a million men in two years, and professional instructors are few. Jonathan learned basic drill from a part-time militia officer who held open the instruction manual the whole time, and had exactly two practice shots with his musket. Luckily the First Sergeant of Company K is a regular army veteran. 'Old Buster' shepherded his confused recruits through the terrible battle of Fredericksburg last December by a mixture of roughness and encouragement. The 20th Maine 'stood fire' as well as any raw unit; and not too many of them lost heart and 'skedaddled' for home during the miserable January march in the rain and mud of the Rappahannock crossings.

During that first campaign Jonathan had little idea what was going on. He recalls a dry-stone wall lined by 'Reb' riflemen, flashing with fire and hung with smoke. In this war infantry rarely stand to meet attacks in the open, but sensibly take—or build—what cover they can. Running towards the wall, the Maine boys lost many comrades.

Afterwards Jonathan found he had rammed three cartridges down his musket without firing—and one was rammed in bullet first, with the powder on top! While wearily drawing them out with a cork-screw tool on his ramrod under 'Old Buster's' cynical eye, he had plenty of time to be grateful he hadn't pulled the trigger and blown his gun—and his head—to pieces.

He has discovered that there is little romance in war. He is embarrassed to recall how he posed in a Portland photographer's studio for a heroic portrait when first issued with his uniform. It was unimpressive at best; and Rappahannock mud and Pennsylvania dust have left their mark since then.

Uniform and equipment

The jaunty visored cap of Government blue may shade his eyes, but becomes shapeless in rain, giving no real protection. The plain 'sack coat'— a simple jacket—is of the same blue wool. It is sturdy—much too sturdy for this muggy summer heat—but it fits his skinny frame only approximately. Heavy wool trousers and laced leather 'brogan' shoes complete the outfit. The trousers, sky-blue when new, are now faded nearly grey. The uniform has no coloured 'facings', no laced loops or regimental cap-plates. The rapid enlistment of hundreds of thousands of temporary soldiers has given the Government no time, money or reason for fancy trappings.

One good thing about campaigning is that Jonathan and most of his friends have 'lost' the uncomfortable knapsack. They still carry nearly 50 lbs of equipment, but it is handier to sling the bulkier items

The Springfield 'rifle-musket'

This is far deadlier than the smooth-bore flintlocks still carried by some unlucky Southern units. The 1861 Springfield 'rifle-musket' is 4ft 7½ins long, weighs nearly 9lbs, and has a calibre of more than half an inch. It is still loaded by ramming a paper-wrapped powder charge and lead bullet down the muzzle; but the bullet is conical, and the barrel has spiral grooves—'rifling'—up the inside. The explosion makes the bullet expand, gripping into the grooves; it spins as it flies, giving a straighter line, and the point is always towards the target. This is much more accurate than the tumbling flight of a round ball from an unrifled smooth-bore. Instead of a tricky, short-lived flint it is fired by a percussion-cap. A little steel tube passes from the breech end of the barrel to the outside of the lock, and over this is placed a copper explosive cap, shaped like a top hat. Firing the gun drops a hammer on to the cap; it explodes, sending sparks down the tube to the powder of the cartridge. It is simpler to use than flints and loose priming, and usually Jonathan can fire even in wind or rain. A practised man can kill with every shot at 300 yards—though as 'Old Buster' says, not one in twenty of the Maine boys are practised enough 'to hit a bull's backside with a fence-rail!' Since they usually fight at close range against whole units of the enemy, this doesn't matter too much. At 50 yards even Jonathan can't miss.

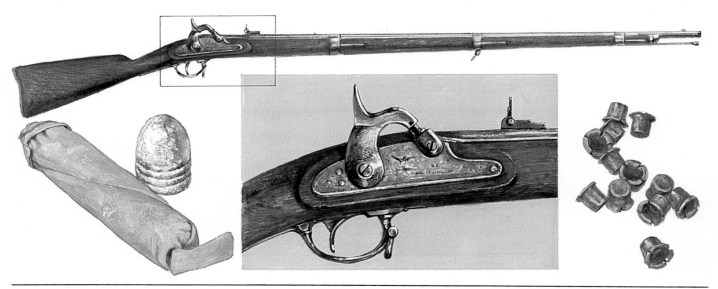

Jonathan Wilkes' equipment:

1 Spare clothes rolled in blanket, tent-cloth and 'gum blanket'. **2** Cartridge pouch; tin containers hold '40 dead men'; brass plate weights flap, prevents loss when running with flap unfastened. Small pocket holds musket tools. **3** Percussion-caps, held and kept dry by sheepskin lining. **4** Tin 1¼-quart canteen with inked initials, unit number. **5** Triangular-section socket bayonet, 18ins long. **6** Mugs were used both for drinking and for boiling up coffee or soup. **7** Ration-bag inside haversack, usually with three days' rations: bacon or beef; 'hard-tack' biscuits; paper or cloth screws of coffee, salt and sugar; fresh vegetables when available. **8** Personal belongings: 'eating irons', Bible, writing kit, 'housewife' of needles and thread, portrait photos of family, razor-case, knife, etc.

round the body in a 'horse-shoe roll' of cloth. In the middle of this are two shirts, lovingly sewn by Jonathan's mother and sisters, and spare trousers. These are rolled in his wool blanket. Round this goes his 'shelter-half', a piece of tent-cloth looped and button-holed at the edges. When they camp, Jonathan and brother George fix their halves together and make a little two-man tent with their guns and bits of cord. Wrapped round the whole roll is Jonathan's most prized item, his 'gum blanket'. This rubberised waterproof cloth makes a groundsheet in camp, and, when he sticks his head through its central slit, a rain-cape on the march. Jonathan is experienced enough to know that a wet soldier on a winter march is prey to illness, and illness kills twice as many men as 'Reb' bullets.

Only one spot of colour enlivens Jonathan's drab uniform. A few months ago the Union Army ordered men to sew simple coloured patches on caps or jackets to distinguish the different Divisions and Corps of the army. The 20th Maine serve in the 1st Division, 5th Corps, and wear a red Maltese Cross. It makes a little scarlet splash on Jonathan's breast. It is just as well he was raised with the 19th century's respect for science and reason; otherwise he might feel it was a bad omen. Of every four men who fight during the three days of Gettysburg, one will be killed or wounded.

Infantry charging enemy behind cover suffered heavy losses. 'Pickett's Charge' at Gettysburg, on the third of July 1863, lost about 6,000 of 11,000 men, with first wave almost wiped out.

1 Walking from 650—350 yards' range; time, 3½ minutes; allows defenders 7 cannon shots (shrapnel shells over 500 yards, solid balls under); also 7 rifle volleys, mostly ineffective.

2 Fast walk, 350—100 yards; 3 minutes; 6 or 7 cannon shots of 'canister', like giant shotgun, sweeps away whole groups; also 6 or 7 increasingly effective rifle volleys.

3 Charge, 100 yards to contact; 40 seconds; 2 discharges of 'canister', 1 or 2 rifle volleys, all devastating at this range.

Corporal Sandor Horthy, 3rd Battalion, 1st Foreign Regiment, 1906

Cavalrymen who fought alongside Jonathan Wilkes at Gettysburg were issued with the first generation of repeating rifles. By the time Jonathan was an elderly man, enormous technical advances had put repeating weapons of great sophistication into the hands of most of the world's footsoldiers. Since the nations which produced them were at a high tide of colonial expansion, the end of the 19th century saw huge empires in Asia and Africa won and garrisoned by soldiers who resembled in many ways the legionaries of Rome 2,000 years before. Badly paid, hard-driven, and still enlisted mostly from lack of any other paying work at a time of industrial change, they were regarded by the rich societies whose wealth and safety they protected as simply brutal, drunken thugs. The conditions under which they served were so grim and monotonous that brutality and drunkeness were often inevitable.

It was mid-morning on the fifth day of the march from the Colomb-Béchar railhead when the company came in sight of the palm-grove. A tiny streak of dark green in the pinkish-brown immensity of the Sahara, it owed its existence to a short stretch of the sluggish Guir river which seeped through the rocks and sand for a few miles before disappearing underground once more. Tiny as it was, this little patch of green was an essential way-station on the almost invisible network of camel trails which had carried the trade of North-West Africa for thousands of years. It was on a rocky knob above the oasis that Governor-General Lyautey had ordered the Foreign Legion to establish a post, as part of his patient campaign to expand French influence westwards from Algeria into Morocco.

The stone-and-mud fort, baked as dry and pale as

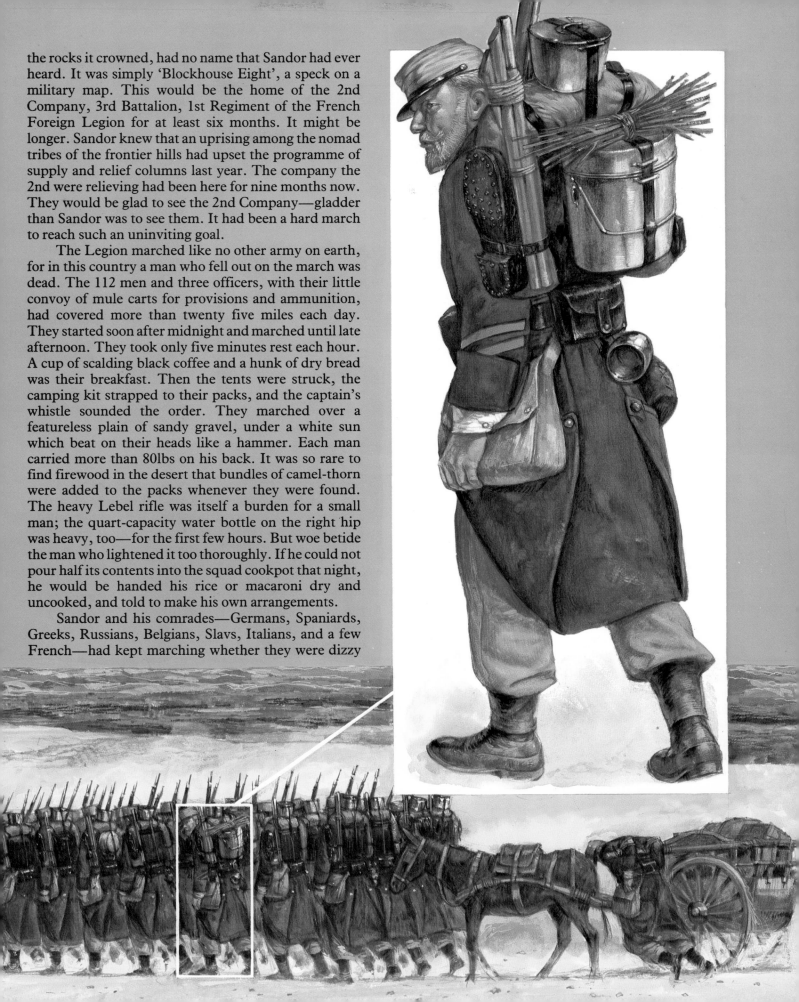

the rocks it crowned, had no name that Sandor had ever heard. It was simply 'Blockhouse Eight', a speck on a military map. This would be the home of the 2nd Company, 3rd Battalion, 1st Regiment of the French Foreign Legion for at least six months. It might be longer. Sandor knew that an uprising among the nomad tribes of the frontier hills had upset the programme of supply and relief columns last year. The company the 2nd were relieving had been here for nine months now. They would be glad to see the 2nd Company—gladder than Sandor was to see them. It had been a hard march to reach such an uninviting goal.

The Legion marched like no other army on earth, for in this country a man who fell out on the march was dead. The 112 men and three officers, with their little convoy of mule carts for provisions and ammunition, had covered more than twenty five miles each day. They started soon after midnight and marched until late afternoon. They took only five minutes rest each hour. A cup of scalding black coffee and a hunk of dry bread was their breakfast. Then the tents were struck, the camping kit strapped to their packs, and the captain's whistle sounded the order. They marched over a featureless plain of sandy gravel, under a white sun which beat on their heads like a hammer. Each man carried more than 80lbs on his back. It was so rare to find firewood in the desert that bundles of camel-thorn were added to the packs whenever they were found. The heavy Lebel rifle was itself a burden for a small man; the quart-capacity water bottle on the right hip was heavy, too—for the first few hours. But woe betide the man who lightened it too thoroughly. If he could not pour half its contents into the squad cookpot that night, he would be handed his rice or macaroni dry and uncooked, and told to make his own arrangements.

Sandor and his comrades—Germans, Spaniards, Greeks, Russians, Belgians, Slavs, Italians, and a few French—had kept marching whether they were dizzy

In the Foreign Legion, as in other professional armies of the late 19th and early 20th centuries, the main problem for the isolated units posted along imperial frontiers in more or less desolate lands was boredom. Active campaigns were few and far between. Men looked forward to them as a chance for variety and excitement. Most of the time there were very few facilities for troops in their spare time, apart from alcohol. Troops were allowed only the most limited contact with the local people, since such contact usually caused trouble. Garrisons were kept to a rigid discipline at all times. A pointless and frustrating routine of parades and kit inspections alternated with brutally hard physical labour, in order to deny the soldiers either the opportunity or the energy for insubordination. In all such armies desertion was common, despite harsh penalties after unsuccessful attempts.

with fatigue, parched with thirst, famished with hunger; whether their feet were covered in blisters; whether they had sunstroke, or malaria; whether they babbled in delirium. A man had collapsed on the third day and had been roped to a pole across a mule-cart ever since. The Legion would not leave a man to be found and tortured by the Arabs; but beyond that, he had to look after himself.

At the end of their march they had reached a stone box 100 yards square, in which they would be shut up for months on end. They would leave it only to fetch water from the nearby spring, or to quarry rocks or mix mud-bricks to repair or extend the walls. They would not be allowed to enter the oasis or the native village. They would work like slave labourers, or perform pointless drills and inspections, or—occasionally—make further marches on patrols of the surrounding desert. In the heat of afternoon they would swelter on their canvas cots, staring at the blank mud-plaster walls of the barracks. In the evening they would eat a greasy soup of vegetables and a few shreds of meat, rice, lentils or macaroni. Unless a miracle happened and a Jewish or Cypriot sutler appeared down the trail with his wagon of drink, preserved foods and cheap trinkets, they might not taste anything sweet for six months.

The only relief from the mindless boredom of a remote post in times of peace was drink. This was the frontier soldier's blessing, and curse. A quarter-litre of wine was issued to every man each night. They would pool it, so that one man at least could get drunk. They had nothing on which to spend their pay of a few coppers a week except drink—and if the sutler called, they would blow every penny in one night. If they could stand on parade and do their work, the officers and tough NCOs turned a blind eye. A man had to have some relief from this tedious life; pushing him too hard might cause a mutiny. But if a soldier broke the rigid laws of service, he got no sympathy by pleading drunkenness. He would find himself in a sweltering cell for days or weeks.

The chance of a fight came as a blessed relief from the boredom of post life, but it came rarely. The tribes seldom united to crush the hugely outnumbered garrisons, and had no idea of modern military tactics. Behind stone walls, even behind a hasty rampart of dead mules if ambushed on the march, the European soldiers of this and other colonial empires could usually hold out until a relief column arrived with artillery, or the newly-invented machine-guns.

In France's North African empire, in Britain's Indian possessions, on America's internal frontier with the Red Indian tribes, in fact all over the world where white nations were extending their power throughout the late 19th and early 20th centuries, the picture was much the same. As long as the white soldiers kept their native foes at a distance they could always win, no matter how outnumbered they were. Their weapon was the bolt-action magazine rifle, accurate to hundreds of yards, and loaded with from five to ten brass cartridges at a time. It fired as fast as the soldier pulled the trigger and worked the 'bolt' or re-loading lever. With hundreds of cartridges in their pouches, and officers who led them intelligently, even a tiny unit of Europeans could lay down a volley fire which no native warriors, however brave, could survive.

Very occasionally there were massacres, usually as a result of over-confidence by an incompetent officer who led his men into an ambush. The warriors of Africa, India and America were much better at concealment, tracking and fieldcraft than their white enemies, and sometimes managed to isolate them far from help or supplies. But the colonial armies became skilful at campaigning in the wilderness themselves; for generations this was the only warfare they knew, and the costly mistakes became less and less frequent.

Sandor Horthy, a Hungarian who had got into trouble with the Austro-Hungarian Imperial police through joining a student radical society, had drifted into this life almost by accident. He had worked as a ship's deckhand after fleeing Hungary. One morning after a brawl in a bar he had woken up in a Marseilles jail penniless, jobless, lonely, and tired of his rootless life. The Foreign Legion recruiting office accepted him gladly, and he signed on for five years in a volunteer corps which was beginning to be famous. He had found little glamour, much hard work, a brutal discipline, and some adventure. He had a home, and comrades who did not look down on him for a misspent life. His promotion to corporal after four years gave him a few privileges, and—in a one-company fort—a certain pride and status. He would probably sign on for another five years when his time fell due.

1886 Lebel rifle: simplified diagram of bolt action

1 & 3 Bolt (**B**) unlocked by pushing handle up; bolt pulled back. Empty cartridge of last round fired is thus withdrawn from chamber (**CH**) and ejected. Cradle (**C**) can now rise, aligning next round with chamber. Front bottom lip of cradle stops third round being pushed back under it by magazine spring (**M**).
2 Bolt pushed forward, locked. This forces next round off cradle, into chamber; forces cradle down, so magazine spring can feed third round back on to it; and cocks spring-loaded firing-pin (**P**) inside bolt. Pulling trigger releases firing-pin, which strikes primer built into end of cartridge, detonating charge inside cartridge. Magazine holds eight rounds; when empty it is reloaded with cartridges pushed down and over cradle and forward up tubular magazine against pressure of spring.

Private Albert Binns
11th Battalion,
The Suffolk Regiment
1916

The old colonial professional armies of the European powers—tough, skilful, obedient to an unimaginative code of discipline—were swept away forever in the first months of the Great War. For the next four years huge armies, representing the whole youth of their countries, fought under conditions which the foot-soldier had only encountered before during brief, isolated sieges. New weapons of unprecedented destructive power caused casualties so great that the old idea of massed infantry attacks along a broad front could never again be considered. For Britain the most terrible lessons of the First World War were learned on the first of July 1916, when the British Fourth Army—including, perhaps, a keen young volunteer named Albert Binns—launched an attack on the Somme front.

Albert Binns is twenty years old today, the first of July 1916. In the drizzling pre-dawn darkness some of his pals gave him a share of their rum ration. The double tot of heavy liquor made him light-headed. Now, in mid-morning, after hours of hard work in the open air, he lies on a grassy slope under the summer sky. Earlier, a lark singing above this rolling downland countryside of Picardy reminded him of the Cambridgeshire fields where he used to work, for ten shillings a week, as a farmboy. Even if the lark's song could rise above the gunfire he could not hear it now. He died an hour ago, gratefully.

Albert was always lucky, and today his luck held good. With three machine-gun bullets in his chest it took him only half an hour to die. No stretcher-bearers could reach the barbed wire where he hung only yards from the enemy lines.

Before the attack he had been told that the week-long British artillery bombardment would destroy the German wire. This was always the key to any chance of success, for if the wire was intact the infantry could not

get into the enemy trenches to capture them even after surviving the perilous crossing of No Man's Land. This time the 'Tommies' were assured that such a weight of explosive was to be dropped on the German lines that the wire would be cut to pieces, the machine-guns smashed and buried, the outnumbered defenders killed or terror-stricken.

In fact, the wrong type of shells had been used. Many of them turned out to be duds anyway. In most places along this sixteen–mile Somme front the wire remained intact. In most of the German trenches the defenders survived the shelling in their dug-outs, cut forty feet down into the solid chalk. When Albert and the rest of the British 4th Army began their dreamlike walk across No Man's Land, the enemy stumbled up from their tunnels, manned their battered trenches, and a thousand machine-guns set up a deadly crossfire. Most of the 57,470 British soldiers who fell on that one day never even saw a German.

Back in September 1914, Albert had counted himself lucky when Lord Kitchener, Minister of War, appealed for a 'New Army' of civilian volunteers. Everyone believed 'it would all be over by Christmas,' and everyone was eager to get into uniform and 'do his bit' before it was too late. Kitchener called for 100,000 men; in three weeks he had 500,000. Albert Binns, tired of the plough and fired by patriotism and a spirit of adventure, was accepted by a grinning recruiting sergeant in a Cambridge church hall. The Cambridge Battalion was a 'Pals Battalion', one of many formed from friends, neighbours, and workmates pledged to serve together. It seemed a fine idea in 1914. In 1916, when postmen brought the dreaded War Office death telegram to whole streets of little houses on the same day, the idea seemed less good.

The Cambridge men, officially accepted into the Army as the 11th Battalion, The Suffolk Regiment, had a chaotic training. For months there were no uniforms, no rifles, and no experienced officers. With unbounded enthusiasm for this 'lark', Albert and his mates were taught the rudiments of drill, musketry, and open-order fighting by elderly veterans of colonial campaigns. In 1915 they arrived in France and were fed cautiously into the front line.

After the first frantic weeks of manoeuvring, in August-September 1914, the armies had staggered to a halt facing one another from parallel lines of defensive positions. These had soon joined up into a continuous belt of trenches scarring Europe from the North Sea to Switzerland. By the time Albert arrived the war zone had taken on a nightmare character of its own. It was 450 miles long. Constant artillery bombardment had turned it into a cratered sea of mud. Villages were pounded by the shells into rubble and brickdust. Forests were blasted into a few splintered, skeletal stumps against the wet sky. To move above ground was certain death. The armies dug themselves down into 'rat-runs' in the wet earth, and there they stayed.

The German Army, secure on enemy soil, could afford to sit tight and wait for the enemy to attack them. Three men with a machine-gun, hidden and protected by sand-bags full of earth, barbed wire entanglements, concrete and sheet-steel, could stop a whole attacking infantry regiment. Ten guns, skilfully positioned, could hold an entire division of twelve battalions at bay in No Man's Land and inflict terrible casualties. The

Albert Binns's equipment:

On the first of July 1916 even first assault waves carried up to 75lbs: half a man's weight, far too much for easy movement or fighting.

1 Steel helmet, cloth non-reflecting cover. Issued from early 1916, it prevented many splinter wounds but not direct hits by bullets.

2 Leather 1914 equipment worn by 'New Army' due to shortage of 1908 webbing set. **3** Two cotton bandoliers each of 50 cartridges; belt pouches held another 100. **4** SMLE ·303in rifle—simple, strong, accurate. Magazine held 10 rounds: trained men fired 15 aimed shots per minute. With bayonet, more than 5ft long, nearly 10lbs weight. (**5A,B**) Head, haft of entrenching tool. Inadequate for heavy work; pick or **6** shovel also carried.

7 Haversack—tin on flap for quick identification by men behind. **8** Groundsheet. Inside haversack: **9** Mills grenades, passed to platoon 'bombers'. **10** Empty sand-bags, filled for repairing captured trenches. **11** Towel; 'holdall' for washing and eating kit. **12** Dry socks: constantly wet feet caused crippling infection. **13** 'Bully beef', biscuits. **14** Mess-tin in cover. **15** Quart water bottle. **16** Bag with two Phenate-Hexane anti-gas hoods; man inhaled through impregnated cloth hood, exhaled through tube.

17 Wire-cutters. **18** British units in 1916-18 adopted simple coloured cloth patches for quick identification of battalion within brigade and division —the origin of modern shoulder-patches. 11th Suffolks wore yellow loop round their shoulder-straps. Many other units at first wore patches on back beneath collar —identification by following attack waves was most urgent. **19** For quick 'trench raids', usually to identify enemy facing them, troops used improvised clubs and knives as well as pistols and grenades; rifles and bayonets were too clumsy for hand-to-hand fighting in the cramped confines of trenches.

Allied generals watched it happen again and again.

The generals, elderly men, could not grasp that the laws which had governed their training and military careers had become irrelevant. To them, war had always been a matter of skilled manoeuvre and counter-manoeuvre by masses of horse, foot, and guns. It was a matter of directing brave men with 'attacking spirit' according to principles which had not really changed since Napoleon's day. They never did understand that the machine-gun made acts of daring almost obsolete, or even foolhardy. They continued to believe that this dishonourable interlude, this business of ignoble cowering in holes in the ground, was a temporary frustration. All the men had to do was to break through the enemy's front line in the traditional way. Then the cherished cavalry divisions would pour through the gap, and 'proper soldiering' could be resumed. Since there was no way to outflank an enemy line 450 miles long, the war settled into a pattern of futile frontal attacks. Between these attacks, the battlefield was ruled by the artillery.

Albert Binns and his battalion served in the British front line trenches for spells of four days to a week. The rest of the time they were marched back to reserve positions in half-wrecked villages a few miles behind the front. The artillery of both sides, positioned in these rear areas, divided their time between shelling the enemy trenches and shelling each other.

Even when Albert was in a 'quiet' sector of the trenches about twenty shells might fall near him during each of several hours a day; when there was a 'hate on', he cowered under constant, deafening shellfire for hours or days at a time. He soon learned to distinguish the sounds of the different kinds of shell, but the knowledge did him no good, since he could not move out of the way. He had to stay in his trench, pressing himself against the front wall of earth and sand-bags, praying the shells would fall somewhere else. When they did, he often saw friends blown to pieces, or horribly wounded by the jagged, red-hot splinters. Even when none fell near him, he found that the constant fear and tension of waiting and hoping was exhausting. He often fell deeply asleep after undergoing shelling. In 'quiet' periods his battalion lost a constant trickle of two or three men a day from the random shelling, and from the fire of expert German snipers who shot anyone careless enough to show their head above the parapet. Heavy shelling might cost a unit a quarter of its strength in a few days.

Even without enemy action the daily life of the trenches was miserable enough. In the constant and nauseating stench of unwashed men, smoky braziers, human waste, rotten sand-bags, disinfectant and unburied corpses, men lived for days and nights in crowded eight-foot-deep ditches. When it rained—and it seemed always to be raining—the duckboards under-

The most striking example of the old-fashioned attitudes of generals in 1914 was the training and equipping of the French infantry for fearless bayonet charges, whatever terrain, enemy or weapons they faced. The glittering wave of bayonets and fluttering pennants were supposed to 'dominate the morale' of the enemy. German machine-guns, having no morale to dominate, were not impressed; in 1914–15 tens of thousands of Frenchmen died, heroically but pointlessly, charging over hundreds of yards of open ground. Their jaunty uniforms looked wonderful but made easy targets. In this respect the lesson was learnt; in 1915 an inconspicuous 'horizon blue' outfit was issued, and soon afterwards the first steel helmets.

foot wallowed in two feet of soupy slime. Albert was usually wet, tired, cold, and on edge.

Sometimes he worked all night. He filled sandbags to shore up the crumbling trenches. Sometimes he stumbled back and forth through the communication trenches, laden with stores. The worst nights were spent on patrols or wire-repairing parties, out in the treacherous darkness of No Man's Land. Here he froze and prayed at every sound lest it attract a German flare, and the machine-gun fire which would follow. Each dawn and dusk the whole battalion lined the firing-step along the front wall of the trench for an hour—these were the favourite moments for an enemy attack.

By day Albert would try to snatch a few hours' sleep. He would curl up under his sodden blankets in a muddy niche scraped in the trench wall. His food was hard biscuit, corned beef, tinned stew that was mostly turnip, or stale bread and the endless plum-and-apple jam. He drank tea made with chlorinated water in old petrol tins. He shared his filthy uniform with a thousand lice, and—worst of all—his blankets with huge, corpse-fed rats.

The 34th Division, made up of three brigades, moved to the quiet Somme valley sector early in 1916. One of the brigades was the 101st, and one of its four battalions was the 11th Suffolks. Albert thought he was 'on a cushy number'. The trenches in this chalky soil were fairly dry and comfortable. No major attacks had yet been made in this area, and No Man's Land was still covered with grass and bright wildflowers. But the days of 'live and let live' were over soon enough. Rumours were followed by orders: a big attack was being planned.

Albert still believed in the war. God was on Britain's side. The 11th Suffolks were the finest battalion in the finest Army on earth. His young officers were kind and enthusiastic. The careful preparations for this attack gave him confidence. When the British barrage began to fall on the enemy trenches, 600 yards away, he felt almost sorry for the Germans.

At 7.30 a.m. on the first of July the barrage fell silent. Led by their young lieutenant, Albert and his pals clambered awkwardly up ladders and 'over the top'. They formed long, orderly lines in the open grassland. Then they began to trudge steadily forward towards the enemy trenches in 'Sausage Valley'. As they walked, the first of those thousand German machine-guns began to rattle, and the 11th Suffolks began to go down in swathes, like mown hay . . .

By nightfall the Cambridge Battalion, of some 800 officers and men, had lost 527—including Albert Binns. The 34th Division, about 9,000 strong, lost 6,380. Total British casualties on that one day were nearly 60,000 men. German losses were about 6,000; little ground was captured.

The First World War went on for another two and a half years after Albert Binns died.

Both sides grew desperate to break the trench-war stalemate. Britain invented tanks to pierce the wire and machine gun nest barriers. Germany perfected new infantry tactics. Instead of whole armies advancing to set plans and timetables, small 'assault battalions' probed enemy defences and pushed on through any weak sectors they found, to reach and knock out artillery in the rear. Strongpoints, isolated and without gun support, then fell to the following infantry. Storm units had practical uniforms, light equipment, but heavy firepower, dragging their own mortars, machine-guns, light artillery, and flame-throwers. Trenches were cleared quickly with showers of grenades, and the first 'sub-machine gun', the Bergmann MP.18. These tactics helped Germany's great advance of spring 1918.

Death in the Trenches

In 1914–18 new weapons, perfected since the 1870s—fast–firing magazine rifles, machine-guns, artillery firing shells of great explosive power over long range with great accuracy—were used by both sides in a major war for the first time. War became so costly in infantrymen's lives that Britain could only replace her losses by conscription: for the first time civilian men were forced into the army by law. Nations which already had compulsory military service had to extend the legal limits; by 1918 schoolboys and middle-aged fathers were at the front. The slaughter so shocked the survivors that by 1939 the generals—who had been young infantry officers in 1914–18—had devised new mobile tactics to avoid the repetition of such horrors. Hundreds of thousands of men died in the trenches. Shellfire and machine-guns took most of them, but thousands also died of disease from the inhuman conditions in which they had to live and fight. That so many fought on, willingly and with courageous skill to the bitter end, shows that men can stand almost anything.

1 Shrapnel shells burst above trenches, hurling thousands of splinters and ball-bearings.

Heavy explosive shells killed whole units, or buried them alive under tons of earth.

4 Sudden trench raids, to take prisoners for interrogation or just to stop the enemy from relaxing, saw vicious hand-to-hand fights with medieval-style weapons.

5 A dreaded trench-clearing weapon, the flame-thrower jetted blazing clouds of oil-droplets long distances, burning men alive.

6 (*Right*) Caught in the open by machine-guns, whole regiments were decimated before they could use their own weapons against dug-in gun cre

2 Many men drowned horribly in the mud, weighed down by their equipment or wounded and helpless. Shells turned the earth to dust; rain turned it almost to quick-sand.

3 Poison gas was spread by shells or on the wind, killing by blistering throat and lungs until men choked to death. Early gas-masks were not very reliable, or always available.

7 After attacks stretcher-bearers heroically searched No Man's Land by night; but thousands of wounded were never found, and died lonely and lingering deaths.

Corporal Joe Borelli US 2nd Armored Division, 1944

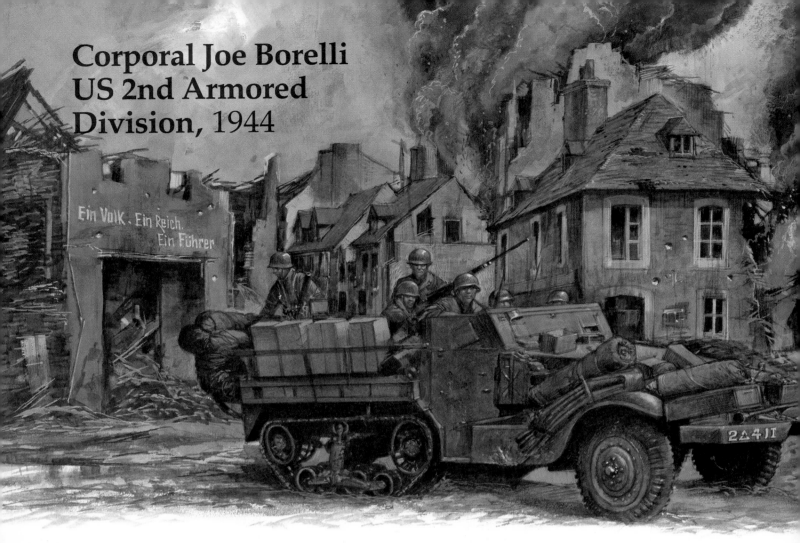

By the outbreak of the Second World War the ordinary footsoldier was not only better armed, better equipped, better supplied and better led than at any previous period in history. He was also—in the free democracies, at least—better treated. Although he was usually a conscript, the nation which put him into uniform was often a stable, civilized society. Its government was subject to the votes of the governed—and the footsoldier and his family were voters. But the peace and civilized standards of his world allowed nations the wealth and technical progress to produce terrible weapons. A young soldier like Joe Borelli was liable to find the ugliness and strain of warfare more distressing than would the young men of an earlier and rougher age.

'Hey, Joe—saddle up! You want to *stay* in this dump?'

Sam Cohen was waving, and beyond him the six remaining members of Joe's rifle squad of 2 Platoon, 'Charlie' Company, United States 41st (Armored) Infantry were clambering into their half-track personnel carrier. On this cold morning of twenty-first November 1944 the ruins of the little German town of Geronsweiler echoed to the squealing tracks and rattling armoured doors of carrier vehicles. They were

driving in from the night leaguer area outside the town to embark the infantry, and take them out again through the rubble-strewn streets still smouldering from yesterday's battle.

Joe remained for a moment slumped on his improvised seat, smoking a cigarette to take away the taste of his breakfast of combat rations. He was getting used to living on the 'C'-ration packages; in this rapid advance, punctuated by daily battles, the company mess-trucks were often prevented from getting close enough to the fighting troops to provide hot food. The ration packs contained chewing gum, candy, cigarettes and toilet paper as well as various canned foods; all these were useful, but Joe thought the processed meat and vegetables tasted like cat-food. There was seldom a chance for fighting troops to heat it properly, and it lacked the bulk a man needed to survive and fight through Europe's worst winter for thirty-five years.

He had spent the night in a fox-hole burrowed into rain-swept rubble. All night, enemy artillery some miles to the east had kept up a random harrassing fire into the ruins. The last few diehards among the German infantry, from whom Joe's outfit had taken the town the previous afternoon, were still lurking in odd corners. Occasional bursts of small-arms fire made it too danger-

ous to light stoves or show a light. The 2nd Armored Division had taken a dozen towns like this in the past few weeks' drive from the Siegfried Line towards the Roer River, and would probably take a dozen more. The defenders were always outnumbered and outflanked, but they usually fought bitterly. The 2nd Armored Division was paying a mounting price.

'C'mon, *paisan*—last train out!'

With a grunt Joe straightened his aching joints and began to assemble his kit. He was dressed from head to foot in the drab, anonymous costume which the power and accuracy of modern weapons forced on all armies for the sake of concealment. The nearest thing to individuality was a scrap of coloured cloth on his shoulder. It identified his division—a group of 10,000 men. For all their drabness, however, his uniform and kit were generally practical and well-made.

His bowl-shaped helmet was in two parts: an outer steel shell which could be used in emergencies as a shovel, latrine, basin or cooking-pot, and a light plastic fibre 'liner' fitted to his head with a web of strapping. Over a thick brown woollen shirt and trousers he wore a weatherproof field jacket. His army was the first to take the sensible step of issuing soldiers with separate garments for battle and for everyday duty. An adjustable harness of strong canvas webbing supported the minimum of necessary kit.

An entrenching tool and a pouch for his aluminium canteen and cup were slung on one hip. On the other was a five-magazine pouch for his ·45in Thompson sub-machine gun: 150 rounds in all. At the front was a small pouch holding a bandage-and-lint field dressing for first aid. Modern medical advances now gave a man a much better chance of surviving even serious wounds, but he had to survive long enough for the medics to reach and evacuate him if he was to benefit from them. Being a prudent veteran Joe carried an extra field dressing pack taped to his webbing, together with a hand-grenade for use in another kind of emergency. His

By 1943 Allied infantry companies had shoulder-fired anti-tank rocket launchers— 'bazookas'. Germany copied these, and in 1944 went one better with the cheap, simple 'Panzerfaust'. **1.**
This one-man shoulder-fired bomb, deadly to tanks at 100 yards, had a built-in 'use-once-and-throw-away' launcher.
2 All armies had mortars in infantry battalion support companies. The British 3-in weapon fired 10-lb bombs between 125 yards and a mile, at speeds of ten per minute.

webbing 'musette bag', handier than the large pack which he left in the personnel carrier with his bedroll, accommodated mess-tins, eating irons, rolled poncho, a box of 'D'-ration chocolate bars, and his few small personal possessions.

Carrying his kit and slinging his weapon on his shoulder, Joe trudged off towards the half-track. He appreciated not having to march everywhere, but was too old a soldier to enjoy riding the vehicle in the front line. It was a big target. It drew enemy fire like a magnet, and it was too noisy for him to hear in-coming fire. Its thin armour and open top could not protect him from anything worse than small-arms fire, anyway.

Mechanized infantry

The 2nd Armored Division was typical of the new type of warfare which had been born of a reaction against the trenches. It owed something to both the British tanks and the German 'storm battalions' of 1917–18. It comprised two tank, one artillery, and three infantry regiments, with supporting specialist units, all motorized and all meshed together by radio communications. This balanced array of different weapons, vehicles, and skills could operate almost independently for long periods, and respond effectively to any type of resistance. A weapon of rapid attack, it flowed forward in separated columns, penetrating enemy positions. The separate elements might join up to attack a target from different flanks, or 'leap-frog' past it to cut it off from behind. Ever-changing circumstances were continually reported by radio to the command headquarters. No enemy defenders could hold off for long this flexible, sophisticated attack.

This highly mechanized warfare demanded great resources of money, machinery, and trained men. To keep Joe Borelli's division—one of dozens—moving and fighting took thousands of tons of fuel, stores, ammunition, food, and water in hundreds of truck-loads every day. Since both sides in this war employed

All armies' infantry squads now had at least one light machine gun to support the riflemen; the US ·30 cal. Browning **3** fired 500 rounds per minute, accurate to 1,000 yards.

4 US Marine with flame-thrower; available to most assault troops, they were not standard infantry squad issue. They were used mainly against bunkers and blockhouses, and were so feared that their threat alone often led to surrender— but captured flame-thrower operators could expect little mercy.

The footsoldier's home

Most campaigns of 1939–45 were too fluid for permanent trench-lines, but the danger of artillery, mortar, and air attack required troops to 'dig in' whenever stopping in one place for more than a few hours. One-man 'foxholes' and two-man 'slit trenches' were cold, damp, and uncomfortable, but were the soldier's only home on the battlefield. Most dress and equipment were generally practical, designed more or less successfully for the realities of campaign life: these British soldiers in France, 1944, illustrate general trends seen in most armies:

1 Thick khaki serge 'battle dress', with many pockets, worn in winter with pullovers, greatcoats, or leather jerkins. 2 Badges, officially removed in combat zones, were often retained: 'Dorset' title for 4th Bn., Dorsetshire Regt.; dragon patch of 43rd 'Wessex' Infantry Division; two bars identify second-senior of three brigades within division. 3 1937 webbing equipment featured 'universal' pouches which accommodated several different types of load —bandoliers of fifty rifle cartridges, or Bren light machine gun magazines, or hand grenades. In fact many

men put ammunition in pockets, and used pouches for snacks. 4 Rifle unchanged since 1914–18, but new 8in spike bayonet—just as lethal as the old 'sword', but less useful for camp chores which were its usual function. 5 9mm Sten sub-machine gun: crude, simple, cheaply mass-produced, unreliable, but effective enough at usual short battle ranges. 6 Spare Sten magazine and 7 Mills grenades, laid ready to hand. 8 Rubberised cape, used as poncho or ground-sheet. 9 Small pack for mess-tins, rations, washing kit, etc.; large pack left on unit

transport. 10 Entrenching tool—picks and shovels still needed for heavy digging. 11 Mess-tin. 12 Mug, heating on solid-fuel burner. 13 Gas mask—issued, but gas never used. 14 Torch. 15 Jackknife. 16 Magazines for squad's Bren light machine gun. 17 Sweets, matches, water-purifying kit, etc., all now issue items. Each man was issued 50 free cigarettes a week, essential for morale. 18 Collapsible gas cooker, one per squad, for use when unit field kitchens could not operate.

Anti-personnel mines

An unpleasant new weapon faced by the infantryman of 1939–45 was the hidden landmine. Dense fields of these were often sewn to cover the approaches to a defensive position. They could—with practice—be spotted, and lifted or rendered safe; but the footsoldier in battle was usually too busy to notice the fine trigger-wires, with hideous results. The German 'S-mine' needed only 7lbs pressure to set it off. The igniter lit two fuses: an instantaneous one to a propellant charge, which blew the intact mine about four feet into the air, and a slightly delayed fuse to the main bursting charge, which then exploded at body-height and hurled dozens of steel balls in all directions, killing or maiming anyone within many yards' range. Another type contained just enough explosive to blow a man's foot off —cheap, but effective. The dreaded 'pencil mine' sent a steel rod vertically upwards into the soldier's groin.

broadly the same types of equipment and tactics, and had equally brave and skilled soldiers, the war had lasted five years already.

Yet the sophisticated machine in which Joe rode was simply a means of putting him into battle. He fought in the dirt, like every footsoldier. Yesterday had been typical.

Advancing towards the outskirts of Geronsweiler on a misty day the head of the division's Combat Command B—two Sherman tanks, and Joe's infantry platoon in four carriers—had come under fire. The Germans were well dug into the cellars, back yards, and culverts of the town, with anti-tank guns, machine guns and mortars already ranged on known spots in the approaches. When the leading tank shuddered back on its tracks and burst into flames, Joe had his squad over the sides of their half-track and spreading out into the muddy fields in a matter of seconds. As they did so one man stepped on a German mine laid in the ditch for that very purpose. Joe bandaged the stump of the victim's leg as well as he could, while the platoon medical orderly injected him with a disposable morphine syringe. Then they stuck his rifle upright by his body as a signal to the stretcher parties, and rejoined the battle.

Re-inforcements quickly came up, and a line of men spread out across the fields, lying in the mud and firing at the gun-flashes in the town. The tanks fired

smoke-shells and high explosive. The machine guns on the half-tracks added to the covering fire. On the signal the infantry got up and moved forward, the squads rushing from cover to cover in alternate groups while their machine gunners gave covering fire. 'Charlie' Company was soon out of the beet-fields and in among the houses. Joe and his two fellow squad leaders paid no attention to anything but the enemy in front of them, and the orders of their platoon commander. In this war the weapons were too powerful, plentiful, noisy, and fast for infantry to await tactical orders from senior officers. Trained to respond in certain ways to certain circumstances, they simply followed the drills.

Men against machinery

Joe's eight-man squad went into battle with a fire-power earlier generations would have found incredible. Eight soldiers, led by a twenty-four-year-old corporal from a poor Italian neighbourhood of New York's Lower East Side, had five semi-automatic rifles, accurate to 500 yards, firing eight rounds as fast as a man could pull the trigger and release it; two BAR automatic rifles which could put twenty rounds into a target half a mile away in just two and a half seconds; Joe's own large-calibre sub-machine gun, firing ten big ·45in bullets a second, highly effective at 100 yards; and between them perhaps two dozen hand-grenades, each capable

of killing every occupant of a medium-sized room. For all these weapons plentiful ammunition was supplied, the men being encouraged to fire off as much as they wished, simply to keep the enemy's head down.

The forty-man platoon of which the squad was part had a heavy squad with two belt-fed light machine guns; and two bazooka rocket-launchers which could turn a tank into a blackened oven, or blast open the corner of a house to silence a sniper. One of the five platoons of 'Charlie' Company had three heavy mortars, each of which could fire a 6lb explosive bomb to any range between 100 yards and one and a half miles, at a rate of one every three seconds; and two more anti-tank launchers. If the young captain leading the company thought it necessary he could radio from his rifle-pit in the rubble for more support—and call down yet more mortar fire from the battalion's support company, or a heavy artillery barrage from the accompanying part of the divisional artillery regiment. A platoon of four tanks supported every yard of his company's advance, their 76mm cannon blasting machine-gun nests, their huge bulk smashing open the enemy's hiding places, their machine guns searching the ruins. The infantry co-operated with them, keeping the German tank-killer teams with their short-range bazookas from closing with the tanks. If the enemy tried to re-group in the open beyond the town, the Combat Command leader could call down 400-mile-an-hour aircraft to smash the attempt with cannon-shells, rockets and bombs.

A hundred years before, an infantryman was safe from the enemy until his officer marched him almost within shouting distance of a specific, visible enemy regiment. Now the danger of death spread for many miles, each side of a front line which the swarming motor vehicles could shift, in any direction, without warning. A man could die as easily from a shell fired five miles away as from an aimed bullet.

Yet the dangers of close-quarter fighting were bad enough. Joe had survived eighteen months' active service in Sicily, Normandy, France, Belgium, and Germany only by watching other men make fatal mistakes. He was now a crafty and experienced fighter. In Geronsweiler his squad drew on his expert knowledge to clear a street house by house, 'mouse-holing' their way from attic to attic all down the row and clearing the other floors from top to bottom with grenades and automatic fire. Joe knew just where to place his BARs on the flank so as to give his attacking riflemen maximum covering fire right up to the moment of contact. He could distinguish the sounds of different weapons in the din of battle, gauging angle and distance, and thus knew how many seconds he had to get his men under cover. He knew where to expect snipers, mines and booby-traps, and how to counter them all. This corporal displayed several times each day the sort of initia-

In 1939–45 infantry fought all over the world, with clothing and kit to match the conditions. The Russian infantry **1** were at first much better equipped than their German enemy. Snow-camouflage suits were worn over warm, quilted uniforms and felt boots. Wide issue of simple sub-machine guns encouraged aggressive close-quarter tactics: such weapons use short-range pistol ammunition. Germany's *Afrika Korps* **2** had well-designed tropical uniforms for desert warfare, both neat and practical. By now most NCOs commanding infantry sections of eight to twelve men, in most armies, carried sub-machine guns instead of rifles.

tive, decisiveness, and responsibility shown a century before by few regimental colonels. The price of this acquired skill was that he was steadily approaching complete nervous collapse.

There was simply no such thing as 'getting used to combat'. Each day the strain got worse. If he lived long enough, it was medically inevitable that in the end—statistically, after about 200 days in battle—he would suffer a nervous breakdown. The symptoms were already starting to appear. He was getting dull and lethargic, and his memory was failing him. He got little value from the few hours' sleep he managed to snatch. His appetite was bad, and he suffered headaches. His eyes had an unfocussed stare. Each time he found himself momentarily safe from the enemy's fire, it took a more superhuman effort of will-power to get up and start moving again.

The only thing that had kept him going this long was loyalty and concern for his close buddies. Each day even this prop for his self-control was being whittled away. Good divisions were too few to be pulled out of the line for a proper rest; they were kept in battle, being 'topped up' with raw replacements as they suffered casualties. By November 1944 only Joe and Sam Cohen remained in the squad from the men who had landed in Normandy in June; in the whole platoon only Joe and three other men remained who had fought in Sicily in May 1943.

Huge as this army was, it was dangerously short of fighting footsoldiers. Statistically the chances of a combat infantryman being hit were as bad as they had been in 1914–18. The new machines of war, and the massive and complex supply organization behind the front line, swallowed up so many of the conscripts that only one in every five US soldiers in Europe was a footsoldier—yet the infantry suffered two out of every three casualties. Training had been cut from a year, in 1941–42, down to a bare three months. Some of the teenagers they were sending to Joe's squad could hardly handle their rifles safely. Joe was tired of getting friendly with a new man, only to see him carried off in a blood-stained poncho. He tended to keep himself to himself these days.

Joe Borelli loved America, and all it stood for. He believed that Nazism was an evil which had to be crushed. The army had taken him against his will, but he did not really resent that too much. He came from a civilized society. As far as was possible in wartime, it treated its soldiers decently. He was quite well paid, clothed, armed, fed, and cared for. If he was wounded he would get excellent medical attention and, at the worst, a good pension.

But Joe was very tired of being cold, wet, exhausted, and frightened. He longed to be back on East 12th Street, safe and warm, surrounded by his family. He really didn't know how much longer he could take this war . . .

Expert Japanese snipers **3** with tree-climbing aids, elaborate camouflage, and rifles with telescopic sights caused many Allied casualties. Paratroopers, like this US soldier **4** had to carry most necessities for several days'

fighting in their own kit when they jumped. Their combat uniforms usually had big pockets for rations and extra ammunition; and weapons were lightweight, often with folding butts for ease of handling when parachuting.

Footsoldiers since 1945

Only rarely since the Second World War have large conventional armies clashed in major wars. Most conflicts have been either short 'hit-and-run' affairs, limited by the enormous cost of modern weapons and equipment; or 'brush-fire' wars in Asia and Africa, involving what are really 'scaled-up' guerilla tactics. Advanced Free World nations cannot afford large standing armies; most rely upon small regular forces,

and limited military training for all young men, recalling them to serve only in emergencies. Pay, equipment, general welfare, and leadership are all greatly improved. Recruiters must compete with civilian employers, and in informed democracies voters demand decent treatment for sons and brothers. In battle, however, the soldier faces undiminished hardship and danger.

American infantryman, Vietnam, late 1960s

Many of the hundreds of thousands of conscripts sent to this distant Asian war for one year each fought with skill and courage. But, for the first time, television showed civilians war's ugliness, turning public opinion against the war and sapping the morale of the troops. Lavishly provided with the most sophisticated weapons and technical aids, commanders sometimes relied upon using them from a distance instead of risking casualties by sending footsoldiers into the enemy-held jungle for long periods. Many local civilians supported the Communist enemy, making the task harder. Unable to rely on massive firepower or air support, the enemy had local knowledge, courage and good fieldcraft on his side. This GI, expensively trained, equipped, and transported, armed with a sophisticated high-velocity M16 rifle and a rocket-launcher, has been put out of action by a device Timocrates of Athens might have thought crude—a pointed stick in a hidden pit.

French paratrooper, Algeria, 1950s

Against determined guerilla enemies supplied by hostile nations, the conscripts who formed the bulk of Western armies could achieve little more than a static defence. Recognizing this, some armies groomed crack units of keen volunteers—often paratroopers and 'commandos'—as a mobile reserve for offensive operations wherever and whenever the elusive enemy was located. Remarkable standards of toughness and skill were achieved, and many such units have indeed proved to be very formidable soldiers. Some observers feel that such élites have drawbacks, however; by 'creaming off' the best available men they may lower standards in the rest of the army.

Vietnamese guerilla, 1960s

Since 1945 Asian Communist guerillas have fought much more sophisticated Western armies with great success. Their victories have been due partly to skill in hit-and-run tactics in sheltering jungle terrain, and partly to dedication. Seeing himself as an elusive champion of the local people against oppression, the volunteer fights out of political conviction rather than for pay. He is a master of concealment, of ambush, of swift attack on isolated targets followed by swift retreat before the less-flexible enemy can react. Without the lavish equipment of advanced armies, he has learned to keep going with simple and improvised kit. Armed with the cheap, sturdy Russian AK-47 automatic rifle, and equipped with little but a bag of rice and a water-bottle, the Vietcong guerilla managed to out-fight and out-last much stronger but more unwieldy enemies. There is no 'magic' about this type of insurgent or infiltrator, however; without the sincere support of the majority of local civilians, he can be beaten decisively.

British soldier, Ulster, 1970s

With the spread of urban terrorism, armies are often needed to support civilian police. Losses to enemy action are not high by wartime standards, but the constant risk of ambush combines with long stretches of boredom to wear down men's nerves. Under provocation, even the most disciplined and restrained troops suffer great tension. As 'sitting targets', such troops are issued with bullet-proof body-armour.

Third World soldier, 1970s

Unhappily, the soldiers of some emergent countries are armed political thugs rather than defenders against outside attack. They are instruments used by many ramshackle regimes to tyrannize their own people. They sometimes live by armed robbery from civilians, since their pay is uncertain. Usually very poorly trained and disciplined, they fight armed enemies only during political coups—rarely in 'wars' as we understand the word. Often out of bravado they copy the outward trappings of famous foreign units. In short, they are modern versions of a type seen all over Europe some 350 years ago.

Warsaw Pact infantryman, 1980s

The footsoldiers who are now being trained, on both sides of the Iron Curtain, against the possibility of war between the Free World and the Soviet bloc, have the same basic mission as their ancestors down the ages. No matter how long the range and how destructive the power of modern weapons, no matter how sophisticated the electronic 'robot' aids, no matter how widespread the use of armoured vehicles and aircraft, in the end the footsoldier will have to walk forward, weapon in hand, and physically take possession of the enemy's territory. The oldest, simplest element in the history of warfare, the footsoldier, will continue to be essential to its conduct for as far ahead as we can predict. But the stress and exhaustion which modern techniques impose upon him are so great that some experts doubt that any future all-out war between major armies can last more than a few days or weeks.

The footsoldier must now fight cocooned in a proofed overall—hot, tiring and intensely uncomfortable—which is supposed to protect him against nuclear radiation and chemical weapons. He must breathe through a respirator to protect him from gases more lethal than any known on the Somme, peering around him through foggy glass goggles. He must ride from safe bases directly to the hell of battle enclosed in a tracked armoured carrier, cramped and confused. He is an anonymous conscript, ordered by remote powers to fight and die for a cause he may not understand or support. He has come a long way, indeed, from the brave, athletic, cultured Athenian marching willingly into battle among his friends and neighbours to fight for the city and the way of life which mean everything to him.

Glossary

Auxiliary cohorts: Roman army units of about 500 men, recruited from non-citizens; the rights and privileges of citizenship were among the rewards for completing enlistment.

BAR (Browning Automatic Rifle), Bren: American and British types of light machine gun of World War II. Since the infantry squad was first issued a light machine gun late in World War I, the classic infantry attack involves the machine gunner and the riflemen advancing in a 'leap-frog' fashion, each firing to keep the enemy occupied while the other rushes forwards to the next bit of cover.

Black Watch: famous Scots Highland regiment—42nd Foot—of the British Army, so nicknamed originally from the dark tartan kilts worn by the Highland security companies—'the Watch'—from which it was formed.

Canister: type of missile fired by cannon—a thin tin can full of musket balls or small pieces of iron. The firing of the powder-charge burst the canister in the barrel, sending out the missiles in a shower, deadly to infantry or cavalry at short range.

Chelsea: the Royal Hospital, Chelsea, founded by King Charles II in the 17th century to care for old soldiers.

Clothyard arrow: the shaft of an English arrow of the Hundred Years' War was, supposedly, of this measurement, the yard as reckoned in the making and sale of bolts of cloth.

Coat-armour: cloth covering of a knight's breastplate, bearing heraldic designs which identified him and his family.

Cohort: basic unit of the Roman Army, about 500 strong.

Combat Command: one of two parts into which a US Army Division of World War II was split for separate operations.

Corps: either a general term used for any military unit; or, since the last century, a formation of two or more *divisions*.

Division: large formation of units, whose strength has varied greatly in different armies at different times. Usually, two or three *brigades*, each of two or more *battalions*, each of 500 to 1,000 men, make up a division, which thus has between 10,000 and 20,000 men including supporting units such as artillery, etc.

Eagle standard: gilded image of an eagle with spread wings, of which each Roman legion had one. Mounted on a decorated pole, it was revered in the same way as a modern unit's flag. In Napoleon's French Army the custom was revived.

Feudal system: name now given to the way medieval European society was organized. Basically, the king was held to own all land, and gave out estates to his noblemen in return for the military service, in time of war, of a certain number of men. The nobles divided their holdings between knights, each of whom was responsible, in turn, for providing a smaller number of men; and so on.

Flare: rocket which bursts over the battlefield and falls slowly, burning with an intense light, to give illumination.

Grapeshot: see *canister*—a similar missile, but with a smaller number of larger balls held together by net or wooden clamps, so resembling a bunch of grapes.

Half-track: type of World War II armoured truck for infantry, with front wheels for steering and tracks at the rear for crossing rough ground; the idea is to enable infantry to go wherever tanks go.

Khaki: drab brown colour adopted for British soldiers' uniforms since the end of the 19th century, and since copied by many armies, to hide men from the enemy; literally, an Indian word for 'dust'.

Legion: main Roman Army unit, of nine *cohorts* each of about 500 men and one double cohort of 1,000. Each legion had a number and a name, and was a permanent unit with a cherished tradition. The term has been used in modern times for various types of unit, because of the great prestige of the Roman legions.

Levy: system widely used for raising temporary armies in early times, usually meaning compulsory service by a set quota of men from a district.

Magazine: metal container of ammunition, with spring to push one cartridge out at a time, either 'built into' modern military weapons, or separate and clipped in place for use.

Militia: local military forces, usually part-time, and sometimes legally excused from service outside the country.

Mills grenade: small hand-bomb, named after inventor, with a short time-fuse ignited by pulling out a safety pin, and a grooved casing which breaks into deadly fragments when it explodes.

Morphine: pain-killing drug, derived from opium.

No Man's Land: the ground between two opposing armies, swept by the fire of both, across which attacks must be launched.

Poncho: soldier's rain-cape.

'Pontius Pilate's Bodyguard': the oldest regiment in the British Army, the Royal Scots (1st Foot), officially raised from an earlier force in 1633.

Roundheads: nickname for Parliament's soldiers in the English Civil War, from the cropped haircuts favoured by some Puritan troops.

Shrapnel: type of shell, named after its inventor, which bursts in the air and showers metal fragments on infantry below.

Sutler: trader licensed by an army to travel in the military areas and sell goods to the troops.

'Tommy': 'Tommy Atkins', the traditional nickname for a British soldier.

Webbing: thick woven cotton belting, used for soldiers' equipment and pouches since the start of the 20th century. It is cheaper than leather, and easier to keep in good condition.